"What does your l... asked.

She ignored the possibilities. "I came here to get some work done."

His gaze held hers. "Work with me."

It sounded like *Live with me, love with me, be with me.* She read all of that in his eyes and heard silent alarms.

"All right," she murmured. "Let's take it slow," she said, watching him in the mirror as he walked up behind her. He placed his hands professionally on her waist, moving her left, right, toward him to the music. On her toes, she leaned in, almost brushing her body against his. Almost. He set her back on her feet, and her heart pounded as if they'd been working for hours.

She dragged her gaze from his, watched the mirror, worked on the patterns. How could she express the emotions of people who'd lost track of how to communicate with each other?

He turned her face to his with his palm, and she looked up in blank surprise. They began again, and never did he hold her any closer than he had to. Even when she clung to him as part of the dance, he simply drew her up and continued the movements. As tension mounted in the music, she was breathing hard. "Stash," she said, watching him, leaning against him.

"What do you want?" he murmured, with movements so precise they expressed none of the desire building deep within. "Tell me what to do."

"Kiss me before I go crazy. . . ."

WHAT ARE *LOVESWEPT* ROMANCES?

They are stories of true romance and touching emotion. We believe those two very important ingredients are constants in our highly sensual and very believable stories in the *LOVESWEPT* line. Our goal is to give you, the reader, stories of consistently high quality that may sometimes make you laugh, sometimes make you cry, but are always fresh and creative and contain many delightful surprises within their pages.

Most romance fans read an enormous number of books. Those they truly love, they keep. Others may be traded with friends and soon forgotten. We hope that each *LOVESWEPT* romance will be a treasure—a "keeper." We will always try to publish

LOVE STORIES YOU'LL NEVER FORGET
BY AUTHORS YOU'LL ALWAYS REMEMBER

The Editors

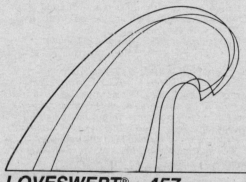

LOVESWEPT® • 457

Terry Lawrence
Passion's Flight

 BANTAM BOOKS
NEW YORK · TORONTO · LONDON · SYDNEY · AUCKLAND

PASSION'S FLIGHT

A Bantam Book / March 1991

ISBN 0-553-44113-2

Published simultaneously in the United States and Canada

PRINTED IN THE UNITED STATES OF AMERICA

OPM   0 9 8 7 6 5 4 3 2 1

One

She moved well. Sensually. Sexually.

He'd expected that.

But he hadn't expected to react this strongly. The way she moved showed him vulnerability, touches of humor. With a turn, a visual caress, she got under his skin, moving like an unchained tigress in the spotlight.

Stash realized then that he wanted her. Knowing himself, he'd have her. Haughty? Perhaps. But if there was one thing life had taught him, it was to pursue what he wanted. To jump. Or, as the Americans would say, go for it.

And he wanted Mariah Heath.

Up there onstage, with a hundred people watching, she danced openly, honestly. She expressed needs frankly, in a way that was more erotic than any shimmying chorus girl, less abstract than most choreographers aimed for these days. Certainly less androgynous.

Stash flexed his foot, then his knee, testing the

familiar pain Mariah's dancing had distracted him from for all of ten minutes. That pain was one of the reasons he was there. He might be attracted to the woman, but he wanted more from her than a sexual fling.

Not that she was making it easy. She was graceful, direct, daring, a romantic perhaps, like him. Stash searched his vocabulary for more words. Compared to Russian, English was so full of words. And what were words anyway when set against her physical presence? She projected all the emotions of a seduction with a flirtatious shoulder roll, a come-hither pout. When she raised her arms, arched her body, and threw her head back, the audience was right there with her, exulting, in love.

So why did Stash get the feeling she was holding something back, protecting something private? He smiled. That was very womanly too.

"Since I fell for you," the tape music crooned out over the enthralled crowd. Mariah played it just right. No self-pity, no shameless wooing of their sympathy. She'd known love, yet knew a real woman didn't curl up and die without it.

But with it? Ah. Stash nursed that thought, imagining, smiling in the dark. He would dance with her—in theaters grander than this cramped off-Broadway space, before thousands, or strictly in private. That's when he knew he'd make love with her. Onstage and off.

He relaxed in his seat, as much as the throbbing in his knee or the pulsing in his lower body allowed. "Mariah." He let her name move on his lips.

She had full round breasts. The spotlight cast

half-moon shadows under the tightened nubs. Her leotard was lightly spangled with stardust and sequins, glittering in the soft pink spotlight that hazed into deeper sunset tones as the song played. Light glanced off her honey-red hair, smoothly pulled back to reveal pale skin and a high, rounded forehead. A wisp of skirt flirted between her legs and swayed out again.

She wasn't in the slender classical-ballerina mold. Overdeveloped was the word Stash sought, but it was wrong. She was undeniably womanly, and she wasn't afraid to show it. The sensuality only added to the turbulent emotions she portrayed in the line of a leg, the crook of an arm.

She was a choreographer but he would approach her as a dancer.

A hollow feeling began in Stash's stomach, the same shallow, empty sensation he experienced while waiting in the wings before a performance. Excitement and challenge, the two things that made life worth living. Change those words to *dancing* and *love* and it would sum up the last ten years of his life. The pursuit of one, the search for the other. He'd never been able to combine them, and the dancing portion of his life was almost over.

He'd known for two years his knee wasn't going to hold out. Too many leaps, too much flying through the air. He had a joke he'd never shared with anyone. "Leaping is all right, it's the landing that's unbearable." And getting more so with every performance.

He had to change; he also had to dance. That meant finding a whole new language of movement. Of all the companies he'd seen, Mariah Heath's embodied the style he'd been looking for: modern and precise, emotive and passionate. All he had to do was talk to her about joining. Tonight. After the performance. Some people would call that rash, but no one had ever called Petr Ivanovich Stashkolnikov cautious.

The love song ended on the long, lonely note of a saxophone. Mariah wrapped her arms across her front protectively. She paced the edge of the spotlight, one foot in front of the other, bare heel to flexed toes. Turning toward the darkness, her back to the audience, she hugged herself tighter, hands splayed over her shoulder blades, an imaginary caress from an imaginary lover. Blackout.

In the context of the song, it got a laugh.

Stash knew it was meant to.

He wasn't laughing.

Mariah scurried into the bathroom at the back of the women's dressing room, and peeled off her leotard as gently as her shaking hands would allow. Stashkolnikov was in the audience! Thank the Lord no one had told her before she went on.

"He was watching *you*," her colleague Constanza insisted in an awe-struck whisper as she scooted out of the cramped room, leaving it to Mariah.

It was a solo, Mariah reminded herself. What else would he look at, the way the backdrop was taped together?

Still, the very thought of him watching her onstage sent tingles up and down her spine. Added to the adrenaline from the performance, she felt decidedly giddy.

She reached into her dance bag for her all-purpose wrinkle-resistant black dress, and grabbed a pair of black stockings and some strappy shoes also. The jeans, leg warmers, and thigh-hugging cable-knit sweater shoved in beside them looked a good deal more comforting. But the dress was for greeting well-wishers after a show, patrons and sponsors of the dance company she'd been working to establish for the past three years. She'd never dreamed one of them might be Stash-kolnikov.

She finished stripping quickly, anything to get out of the grim two-stall bathroom. Industrial yellow paint from another era peeled obligingly to reveal the green beneath. The walls were clammy concrete block, and heaven knew how many cock-roaches resided under the rusting pipes. She'd never had the nerve to look, and if one dared run across her foot, she'd probably hurtle out of there stark naked.

"Twenty-eight is a little late to become claustro-phobic," she muttered. And it didn't help the breathlessness she'd felt ever since she'd heard Stash's name murmured excitedly in the wings. He was there, watching The Movement, her company, her business, her baby. And she had more important things to worry about than being star-struck.

Raising her arms, she slid the black dress over her body. She found a multicolored scarf in the bottom of her bag and tied it around her waist. The hot-pink leg warmers went on over the nylons, a concession to her aching Achilles. She did a few quick circles with her foot, then flexed. A sus-tained stretching session awaited her back at her sublet apartment. "Speaking of cockroaches . . ." she mumbled.

There was a knock on the door. "Next Tuesday at one?" a man called.

Recognizing Danny's voice, she swallowed the heart that had leaped into her throat. "We'll be auditioning for next season," she answered. If they could afford one.

"So be there or be square."

She cracked the door open to peer at the lanky Texan who was her leading male dancer. "You're in and you know it, Dan, but I want to add some new faces."

"Wouldn't miss it." He winked at her as she closed the door, his voice a low conspiratorial whisper through the flimsy panels. "Speaking of new faces, I hear there was one in the audience tonight. *Ciao.*"

Mariah's heart skipped another beat. A corner of her mind wondered if Stash's visit might be worth a mention in their publicity materials. Carefully worded, of course. Grinning ruefully, feeling guilty for even entertaining the idea, she caught sight of herself in the mirror.

As a choreographer, Mariah would do just about anything to see The Movement succeed. Next week's auditions might bring out some new talent, strengthen them overall. She'd long since given up the idea of being the star. Without makeup she could blend right into walls. As pale as redheads got, she was unmarked by so much as a freckle. Her forehead was high, her face a perfect oval. It was a ballerina's face, always had been. It was the body beneath that had been her downfall.

Never mind, she told herself. The nose was small, the eyebrows tweezed but perfect. Her mouth was full and pronounced when outlined in lip liner. But lacking mascara, her lashes were as pale as her skin. Some people kindly suggested that made her big brown eyes stand out even more. Whether it was true or not, Stashkolnikov would decide for himself, provided he was still hanging around.

"Oh, well." She took a deep breath and reminded herself she'd given up being insecure years before. "Nineteen eighty-two, to be exact. January first." Quickly smoothing back her hair, she walked out of the bathroom and into the main dressing area.

He was sitting on the corner of the makeup table, broodingly handsome in black, one leg dangling, toe effortlessly pointed in a black Italian leather shoe. The greatest male dancer in the world looked restless. And breathtaking. At least, that was the reaction of Mariah's suddenly starved lungs. She noted the outline of a muscular thigh beneath the dark slacks.

"Excuse me." She set her dance bag between them on the table and tugged a tissue out of a dispenser. The box came halfway across the table with it. She draped a towel around her shoulders. *Don't gush*, an inner voice insisted. *Don't fall all over yourself. Act normal!*

She cleared her throat and tried a winning smile. "We usually don't allow visitors at this point. Ruins the illusion."

"I know all about illusion." He spoke softly, as if the word held deeper meaning for him. As if it were something they had in common.

Her eyes locked with his and her sense of balance swayed, like a curtain going up on a darkened theater. She was dreadfully afraid she'd already run out of conversation—teasing, rambling, chattering, or otherwise.

"Here." He broke the ice, dipping a finger in a jar of cold cream and dabbing it on her nose. "If we're going to dance together, I should see the real you." He smiled.

How many starlets had fallen for that smile? she wondered. She could see why. If she didn't break this spell, she could also stand there with cold cream on her nose for something like the next twenty years.

She wiped it off hurriedly, and her hand clenched around the cool white jar. "Dance together? Us?"

"It is what I intend," he said with a sharp nod. A lock of black hair fell over his forehead. "However, first I have some criticism I would like to share with you."

Share? He could share just about anything with her. Realizing she was staring, and he was staring back, Mariah plunked the cold cream jar down onto the dressing table and snapped to. "Criticism?"

"Yes. I didn't like, you know?" He demonstrated, wrapping his arms around himself in a bear hug and mugging. "Too easy. Cheap laughs."

Blood rushed to her cheeks, but Mariah found an all-purpose smile to plaster on her face. She fought the urge to glance in the mirror and see if it looked as hideously false as it felt. "Isn't that a little harsh?"

"Harsh you need." He was getting excited, his Russian accent thickening. With a distracted wave of his hand, he tried to explain. "You show so much emotion, act so vulnerable, then you make people laugh. You hide behind this laughter. The other pieces, they were funny, yes, but this one shouldn't have been. You pulled back from the edge, yes?"

Mariah took a sip of water from the glass that waited for her after every performance, and quickly scanned the dressing room. Four other dancers hovered, along with a dozen friends and a couple of men who could very well be from the press. Stashkolnikov was criticizing her in public, and worse, there was a kernel of truth in what he was saying.

She'd had trouble with the ending of that number. She'd felt too exposed. The laugh was easy. It worked. The fact that she'd wanted to replace it was no excuse. "Mr. Stashkolnikov—"

He held up his hand imperiously.

Mariah knew what he was going to say and knew just as surely that she couldn't possibly comply.

"Everyone calls me Stash."

No way, she thought. She'd admired this man since he'd landed on U.S. soil, seizing center stage of the National Ballet Theater as if he were born to dance there. Through a handful of television performances and a shelf full of VCR tapes, she'd watched him dance . . . watched him fly.

Vaguely she wondered what he'd do if she told him she'd had a crush on him for ten years, a full-blown round-eyed heart-palpitating crush any fifteen-year-old would be proud to call her own. But if it was this hard talking to him, arguing with him about a dance number was beyond imagining. "Mr. Stashkolnikov, thank you very much for your advice."

"Bah!" He waved his hand as if swatting flies.

"You put me off with polite phrases." Pacing, he combed his hand through hair so black, spotlights on a hundred stages had been swallowed in it. His eyes, when they turned on her, glittered.

Oh, Lord, she'd insulted him. She thought she'd learned some self-possession as head of her own company. She'd definitely learned that everyone was a critic. "I only meant—"

"To shut me up. Here." He grabbed her shoulders, pulled her up on her toes, and kissed her on the left cheek, the right, the left. "I love your dancing, I love your company. There, for all to hear. You hear?"

Everyone in the group around them chuckled and nodded. Mariah tried not to shrink under the table. She didn't mind being the center of attention, of course, as long as she was the one controlling the time and place. Not with Stash around, though. The man had a way of taking over.

"It's because I have the utmost respect for what you do," he said, wagging a finger under her nose, "that these little things upset me. Now, you come and we discuss privately."

Before she could object, he'd steered her around the makeup table and out into the hallway. Mariah watched the mouths of patrons drop open as Stashkolnikov himself led her past them. Finally they came to a door she'd never noticed. He swung it open. She expected a coat closet. It was a broom closet. "In here?"

"We talk."

"Now, look—"

He had both her shoulders gripped in his hands. She backed in quickly before he got it into his head to kiss her again. These Russians could be volatile.

The door shut behind them with a metallic click. The air was mop-musty. A distinct odor of disinfectant twitched in her nostrils. Then there was Stash. The musk of his cologne seemed to have been imprinted on her cheek, along with the slight rasp of beard from his kiss.

A five o'clock shadow darkened his jaw, making him look slightly disreputable, not clean and sleek like some dancers. Male, harsh, unconstrainable, like one of the darker forces of nature. Like the way her heart pummeled her rib cage as she stood so close to him.

She tried not to listen to their breathing. Folding her arms across her chest gave her some room. The mop bucket pressed coldly against her aching calf, despite the leg warmer. "I'm flattered you take us so seriously that you'd want to offer your opinions."

"That's not all I want to do." If she had any idea, Stash thought with a smile, she'd be doing more than crossing her arms.

She shrugged, a level-headed businesswoman who could take a little heat. "I'm all ears."

She was all something, but ears wasn't the word Stash thought of first. "You dance naked."

The thin arcs of her eyebrows rose. "Pardon me?"

"Naked." His voice rasped, tailor made to match the rasp of his cheek. "I could see everything onstage."

He sensed her fighting not to glance down at herself. "I don't think I'm quite following—"

"Naked is good." Naked was what he needed,

something besides secrecy and carefully calculated statements to the press. Something besides emotions he feared would wither like unused muscles if he didn't find someone to share them with, someone he wasn't sure existed until he'd seen Mariah Heath dance. "You give emotion, you express without hesitation. Physical, sensual. You don't hide."

"Well, yes." She was distinctly unnerved. Those were just the words she called out in rehearsal. *Come on, people, give me the emotion. Don't hide from me.* So why did she feel the need to do just that with him? "Thank you, that's very kind."

She forced herself to look into eyes the color of molasses. The darkness was intense. His wide mouth was set; his cheekbones were carved, savage. She'd read he had Cossack blood. She didn't doubt it for a minute. She shivered.

With a flourish he took off his calf-length leather coat and draped it around her. A plastic bottle of cleanser fell off a shelf behind her and landed with a thunk. The sound her heart was making.

"You'll catch a chill," he said, his voice gruff but tender.

This was definitely fantasy material, Mariah thought, but she knew that on the other side of that door, reality waited. She had a company to get off the ground, a name to establish. There was the small matter of his public diatribe, too, and who were those people in the dressing room? Getting a grip on herself, she clutched the lapels of his coat. "Thank you again for the advice, but I'll catch hell if I don't get back and hobnob with some of our supporters."

She maneuvered past him in the tight space. His hand covered hers on the doorknob.

"I want to dance with you, Mariah. Will you teach me?"

"How to dance naked?" She tossed the remark over her shoulder, amazed she could manage a light laugh.

"You act like a woman, dance like one. Not willowy like a teenager, a girl . . ."

Built like a brick outhouse, one of her dance evaluations had read. She'd been fifteen, in her tenth year as a dancer. And yet the beginning of womanhood had very nearly spelled the end of her career.

The embarrassment stung all over again. So did the injustice. Her body had acted against her will. It had grown up. And out. With Stash's face looming beside hers, the wisp of his breath stirring unpinned hair against her cheek, she knew there were other ways a body could betray a woman.

"Mr. Stashkolnikov, I've thanked you for the compliments *and* the criticism. However, I'm not often abducted from one of my own performances, nor waylaid in a broom closet." She was woefully aware she sounded rude and abrupt, but that didn't change the fact that she needed air, fast. "Shall we say good night?"

She gave the doorknob a crank. Nothing happened. She twisted it again, all three hundred and sixty degrees.

"Perhaps no one uses it from the inside," he said.

Probably not, she silently agreed. It was too small for one person to come in and close the door, not to mention two.

As discreetly as possible, she shoved her shoulder against the door. It didn't budge.

With a clatter, Stash backed into the bucket and mop. "Maybe we could kick it open like police on TV," he said, and actually lifted a foot.

She gasped. "Don't you dare. You'll ruin your knee."

If she hadn't been so intent on the door, she'd have seen the way his features froze. His smile quickly disappeared. "We can't very well be stuck in here," she muttered.

Stash reached over her head and rapped sharply on the door. "Assistance, please!"

The door flew open, Mariah tumbling after it into the hallway and the knot of people who'd gathered around. The formally dressed dance aficionados stopped in their tracks, gaping. Mariah nodded to them as if this were a common after-performance ritual. Smoothing back her hair, re-settling Stash's heavy leather coat on her shoulders, she calmly marched back to the ladies' dressing room.

But not before she glimpsed Stash sauntering out of the broom closet as if it were a first class hotel. She'd bet any one of those startled patrons would have gladly hailed him a cab.

In the dressing room, tossing his coat over a chair and hairpins into a tray, Mariah itched to throw something heavier and a good deal noisier. How humiliating! Not only was Stashkolnikov . . . well, Stashkolnikov, he was also a notorious Lothario. And there she'd been literally closeted with him at the last performance of her spring program!

With the female members of the company long since changed into street clothes, the male dancers wandered in, trading blow-by-blow accounts of the performance, tempered by compliments from those audience members who remained. The critics, if that was who those two men were, were still hanging around. Mariah figured she could get a word in with them if she hurried.

All conversation stopped and every head turned as Stash walked in. His eyes, Mariah noticed with a shiver, were on her alone.

"Perhaps you misunderstand," he said, stopping close to her.

She allowed herself to use his nickname, strictly on the understanding that it would get his attention. "Stash, this may be a joke to you"—or a come on, she added silently—"but I don't know where you got this picture of the two of us getting naked—"

"Miss Heath?"

"Ms. Heath?"

Her stomach plummeted as she slowly turned to the two men standing behind her. She didn't need a mirror to know her cheeks were blazing red. "Yes?" she croaked.

"I'm Greg Tonkin from the *Observer*."

"Bill Davis from *Cityscape*. We'll both be reviewing tonight's performance, and we wondered if we could have a word with you."

"Of course. I'm so happy to meet you." She hastily extended her hand and smiled for all she was worth. Neat trick, she thought. Both men managed to find her hand without once taking their eyes off Stashkolnikov. At least they weren't staring at her chest.

So much for publicity.

Two

"You may have heard of us?" Mr. Davis said.

Mariah had. They didn't represent the biggest papers in town. One of them was barely a supermarket handout, but it had a natty little arts and entertainment section covering SoHo, Greenwich Village, and TriBeCa. Mariah wanted the exposure they could provide. The Movement needed it.

Too bad they'd waited until the last performance to stop by. It was April and her company wouldn't be taking the stage again until fall. Any notice they got from this would surely fade by then. She concealed a sigh. That was the way it went with publicity. By the time word got around, it was often too late.

"I hope you enjoyed the performance," she said.

They nodded, glancing at each other. "Uh, maybe it's eavesdropping, but did I just hear you say you were going to dance together?"

They probably heard more than that, Mariah thought. She took a deep breath and braced herself, balancing evenly on both feet.

Stash pulled her off at least one when he threw his arm around her shoulders and proudly announced that that was true. "I plan on joining The Movement as soon as Mariah and I work out the details."

"What?" She whirled on him, a difficult and clumsy thing to do in his one-armed embrace. She was keenly aware of both men scribbling notes as fast as their pencils could fly. "Excuse us, me, I mean, I'm sure Mr. Stashkolnikov is teasing. As long as I've been acquainted with him, I've never known him to be serious."

"And you've know him for how long?"

"Half an hour," Stash said, grinning from ear to ear. But his dark eyes were unwavering when he turned to Mariah. "If you knew me better, you'd know I never kid about dance," he murmured.

His voice against her ear made her quiver deep inside. Time to pointedly lift his arm and step away. "Gentlemen, I don't want you to be taken in by a publicity stunt or a joke. I'm very serious about my company and we don't need this—"

"You need me."

"Stash."

She'd called him Stash. They wrote that down. The rapid rustling of paper sounded like scurrying mice. Mariah scrambled to undo the damage Stash seemed intent on making worse.

Too late. He stepped behind both men, draped his arms around their shoulders like an old army buddy, and steered them firmly toward the hall. "All I'm at liberty to say, my friends, is that I have been released from my contract with National Ballet Theater as of yesterday."

Gasps greeted that announcement, one of them Mariah's.

"Our parting was mutual," he added.

Cut loose, dissatisfied and edgy, Stash had come there that night looking for something. Who could have predicted he'd find what he needed so desperately, a future in dance *and* a woman to share it with?

Was his action rash? Impulsive? If a man saw a diamond on the street, did he walk around the block a few times before picking it up? Let others question his actions; to him it all made perfect sense. One look at Mariah and he'd done what he'd always done so well. He jumped.

"I wish to climb new mountains," he said aloud.

Nervously tapping a pen to his pad, one of the reporters worked up the nerve to ask, "Does this have anything to do with the knee problem?"

Stash pursed his lips and squinted at a bare overhead light bulb. "Men with knee problems do not climb mountains. I am fine. In fact, I will be reporting to Miss Heath's auditions next Tuesday at one. Yes, I will take class. I have much to learn and I look forward to learning *everything* she has to show me."

That included the woman, he mused. But when he turned to see if she'd gotten the message, he glimpsed no more than the flash of honey-red hair as she flounced out the back door, dance bag swaying like a heavy, rain-wet flag.

He liked that. She didn't hide her temper either.

"I believe it will be a very interesting experience, gentlemen."

The problem with working in New York, Mariah always said, was that The Movement had to be reassembled every season. Since she was unable to pay year-round salaries, some of her dancers got other jobs, joined Broadway shows, or took positions with more established companies. Hence, auditions for extra dancers. Mariah compared it to spring training—who's on the team, who's ready to come up from the minors, who's new in town. The competition also kept her regular corps on their toes.

She climbed the stairs to the rehearsal hall they rented on the third floor of a converted warehouse in lower Manhattan. The space was great, the rent cheap—for Manhattan—and the location reasonable.

The one drawback was the need for a bigger office area. Of course, that applied only if the company survived. In the past three years, their phone lines had hardly been jammed with calls for tickets. Their posters were laid out on the same drawing board where the costume sketching was done. Music and tapes were stored at her apartment. A couple of file cabinets and a desk served as administrative headquarters. They'd barely felt pinched until Stash announced he was joining The Movement.

Joining. She'd read it in every paper published in New York. The phone had been ringing off the hook. Starved for publicity a week ago, she was ironically reduced to a string of "No comment."

Mariah took a deep breath, squared her shoulders, and walked into the high-ceilinged rehearsal room, with its wall of windows on one side and mirrors on the other.

She'd been prepared to meet Stash again. But no one had prepared her for the crowd of dancers vying for spots in the company. She estimated there were at least fifty. In previous years they'd been lucky to draw twenty. Since the company consisted of four men and three women, plus Mariah, she usually winnowed her way through an audition quickly. The day was looking longer by the minute.

" 'Morning, everyone," she called out when she'd recovered from the shock.

A few hands waved as Constanza led the group through some warm-up stretches. Searching out the familiar faces of her regulars, Mariah didn't have to ask why a knot of reporters were buzzing in the corner. Or who they surrounded.

"Welcome to the Moscow Circus," she murmured to herself, setting her bag beside the baby grand piano in the corner. " 'Morning, Janine."

"Did you know . . . ?" Janine her accompanist, had eyes as round as the saucer-size earrings she wore.

"I can read."

"Is he really joining?"

Mariah flipped through a stack of sheet music. "Play us a half hour for stretching, please, then we'll warm up to some Dixieland. Next I'd like to work with the women. Debussy would be nice, but not too tinkly." She stopped when she realized Janine was staring at her.

Janine had been with her for three years, as long as anyone in the fledging company. Her colorful African-print dresses and equally cheerful demeanor brightened up the day-to-day grind of attending class, making the hard physical work seem almost entertaining. Mariah didn't usually underestimate her.

"Sorry. You know the routine. We'll just be limbering up, weeding out some of the extras, and evaluating the newer dancers."

"And him?"

When a TV light on a boom reflected off his black hair, Mariah caught a glimpse of Stash through the crush of people. "He'll audition like anyone else." She smiled with grim determination as Janine gasped.

Striding to the center of the room, Mariah clapped her hands three times, studiously ignoring the melee in the corner. "Okay, people. Now I get to undo the damage all your other coaches have done."

Her methods alternated strict with fun. At this stage she wanted to loosen up their spirits as well as their bodies. As the summer wore on and they met more regularly, she'd be specific about what they could and couldn't get away with. And if Stash thought he could talk through warm-up—

He parted the throng and took his place in the back row with the other male dancers. Staring at him, Mariah lost track of what she was supposed to be doing and had to close her eyes to think a minute. The man looked marvelous.

He wore black tights and a baggy gray T-shirt that delineated the muscles of his chest. A tear revealed a smattering of black hair. A black sweater was tossed carelessly around his shoulders, tied by the arms at his neck.

Street clothes had concealed him, dance clothes celebrated him.

"Let's start easy," she said.

Gauging the mood, Janine began playing slowly in the background. Mariah lifted her arms overhead. The class, and Stash, followed. A dozen flash-bulbs went off. Lean to the right. A dozen more. Mariah sighed and remained calm. Stretching, after all, was supposed to reduce stress.

"Now pick it up, people. We're not doing a weeping-willow exercise."

Disgusted with the quaking in her limbs, Mariah stepped over to the row of chairs against one wall and peeled off her shapeless sweater. Beneath her peach-colored leotard, her nipples were pronounced. Despite the ruddiness flaming her cheeks, it was chilly in the cavernous space. The row of industrial windows might provide wonderful light, but it came with exorbitant heating bills. Mariah grabbed a colorful scarf and tied it around her shoulders like a shawl, then faced the class.

Getting back into the flow, she walked them through a slow-tempo number. Flow mattered. But with Stash there, she was having trouble finding it. So was everyone else. Dancers always looked in mirrors, watching their lines, seeing as well as feeling the elongation of a leg, the arch of a back. But this group was more interested in what Stash was doing. Mariah made a move, Stash copied it, then the dancers followed *him*. It would have been funny if it weren't so nerve-racking. And if he didn't have his gaze fastened on her, beat after beat, measure by measure. He made her feel they were the only two people in the room. Telling herself that intense concentration was the sign of a true professional didn't calm the fluttery feeling in her knees.

Did she really have the nerve to make him audition? Or was *her* company auditioning for *him*?

"As Constanza probably told you," she announced when the warm-up was finished, "we have spots for two new women dancers and three alternates."

Stash did some quick math and interrupted from the back. "Surely you'll dance too."

"I won't be dancing next season."

"That is a grave mistake."

Mariah's mouth thinned. She wasn't used to being second-guessed. It wasn't much consolation that the dancers were finally watching her, or that she had a host of reporters at her back literally looking over her shoulder. She explained patiently. "Heading up a small dance company involves a number of things besides dancing. Choosing music, lighting, costumes. Directing as well as choreographing, as you can see. I even help mail the subscription tickets, something I doubt you had to do at NBT."

Nervous titters among the dancers; a hushed silence in the press gallery.

"I've taught and directed," Stash said, arms folded across his chest, his jaw set.

"That's apparent," Mariah murmured. It went with his penchant for taking charge. She rubbed the ache beginning at the back of her neck. "I simply don't have time to dance. I've been cutting back for two seasons."

"This is wrong. You must!" He knew his insistence might puzzle or even irritate her, but he couldn't explain that dancing with her was half the reason he'd come.

"Mr. Stashkolnikov, I will run my own company, if you don't mind."

Though his emotions dictated otherwise, Stash

didn't cross the space between them. His voice was quiet but forceful, carrying across the expanse of wooden floor. "To dance is like love. As long as you are able, you shouldn't stop. Life gives you only so many chances."

"And life takes them away?" she asked, for a moment forgetting everyone else in the room.

Stash nodded. He'd seized his chance to dance, defecting to do so, paying a price that was still being exacted. Part of it had meant leaving behind those he loved, and thinking twice before he loved again. Did Mariah know that kind of dedication? He suspected she did. Her company was too important to her. She'd made it her life. And his?

Dancing was how he lived, and expressed love. Mariah expressed so much when she moved, he had to believe she understood. It was vital that she did. "You should dance all you can," he insisted.

The flutter in her knees had become a warming heat spanning her veins. Mariah knew better than to pretend it was the exercise. Dance all you can? And what if the shape of her body determined that a life in classical dance was beyond her? Stash had chosen to dance in the West, deciding between classical and modern as his whims apparently dictated. She hadn't been allowed a choice.

Until she'd formed her own company, latching on to a modern style of dance and making it her own. "I'll decide what I do and when, thank you." That settled that.

She stepped briskly over to the piano, covering her retreat with a show of flipping through music. He'd gotten too close, probing areas that remained painful. And as for love . . . There was work to do.

"The publicity has to be great," Janine whispered urgently, fingering a piece of music. The words "don't blow it" were left unsaid.

"Maybe it'll get in *People*," Mariah commented tartly. "One column of type beside a page-and-a-half picture of Stash with his T-shirt sticking to him." Not that she'd noticed.

Perhaps prudence and a little more patience were in order, she thought nonetheless. Far from molding everyone to her vision, she prided herself on being able to meld a group of individuals into a cohesive unit. Stash was just a tad more individual than anyone else.

And more attractive. Heck, she'd buy a copy of *People* if it had that picture in it. A voice in her head chided her. Who was she to mold this man into anything? To instruct him in anything? More to the point, did she dare let him get as close physically as he had emotionally a moment before? If they danced, how could she avoid it?

She dawdled over the music, inadvertently eavesdropping on the conversation starting up among the male dancers seated nearby. It was the usual litany of local jobs and regional workshops, all of it stilted and hushed with Stash there.

"I did *The Nutcracker*," one dancer said.

"Me too," another added. "The company was so small I did three parts. Off in one, change, go on, come off, change, go on again."

A few eyes slanted Stash's way.

He shrugged fatalistically and put on a convincing frown. "You all have the advantage over me. When I danced it last year, they gave me only one role."

Even Mariah chuckled. His "one" role had been

the prince. It had been filmed for PBS, and it won an Emmy.

It also broke the ice. The gushing began.

"You know, I saw you on TV in that the first time you danced it. It's the reason I'm a dancer."

"I've admired you practically since I could walk."

"I saw you in the Balanchine last year. *Apollo*."

Apollo, Mariah thought, No, she'd make him Icarus, seizing his own destiny, escaping confinement. Bold, daring, flying to the sun. That sealed it. The idea that he might dance in a number choreographed by her was too much to resist. This intense awareness of him as a man was something she would simply have to learn to live with.

Clearing her throat, she did the same deep breathing exercises that got her over the hump of stage fright, and stepped back out into the room. Time to ask the greatest male dancer in the world to audition for a company that was barely scratching by. Her company.

"Mr. Stashkolnikov, would you care to dance for us?"

He walked front and center, proud to be asked.

Lord, the way the man carried himself, Mariah thought. Shoulders squared, chest muscles rippling beneath that T-shirt. Thighs and calves honed to artistic perfection. The sheer joy of strength radiated from him. Energy and will and ambition. He broke bonds, flying where others only longed to, herself included.

She felt a twinge of shame. He shouldn't have to do this. She should be on her knees thanking him for the publicity alone.

Another flash went off.

He stood, feet turned out, legs tight together,

muscles delineated in black tights, like a panther waiting to strike. He extended one hand to the female dancers, the other to the males, then he bowed. "May I have the honor?"

Something in Mariah quivered. She squelched it. "Stash. Before this relationship goes any further, I have to tell you—"

"Relationship? Ugh." He made a show of furrowing his brow and shuddering visibly. The company laughed at what was obviously a performance. "Let's not get into those, please."

Stories about his public and very vocal breakup with his latest starlet were still circulating, renewed by this recent rash of coverage.

"I have no time to dance," Mariah repeated, although the words sounded lame, lacking conviction. "At present I have no intention of dancing next fall." It didn't solve the problem of how often she'd need to touch him if he joined the company, straightening a leg, explaining a pose, demonstrating. But it drew a line, and lines, distance, was what she suddenly needed.

His hands behind him, studying the floor, Stash paced off the space, nodding as if in complete agreement. "I dance alone, then." And he did.

Stepping and turning, arms extended as if he held a partner, he swayed to the tentative steps of one of her own pieces, *Rondelay*. He must have seen it at the performance the previous week. She was flattered he remembered it so well.

When he'd completed a circuit of the room, he paused. He placed one foot, drew it back, lips pursed in concentration, then he moved it to the right.

"No." He shook his head forcefully, black hair

falling across his forehead. "It's no good if you won't dance with me."

A part of her danced every time she looked at him, she admitted silently.

"It's the movement, it's—bah!" Words failed him, Stash thought with frustration. His body scarcely ever failed. Ignoring her hesitation, he took Mariah's arm and led her into the ring the other dancers had formed. "Show me how you do this part."

Janine obliged with the music. It was the section when the male dancer put his arms around the female dancer from behind, palm flat against her abdomen, hips brushing hers, thighs tucked behind slightly bent thighs.

The flashbulbs could have been wired to Mariah's pulse.

She'd designed this, she thought, demonstrated it herself to a couple who danced it in performance. How could it suddenly take on a whole new erotic life? Her search for reasons scattered when Stash, in keeping with the dance, ran his hand down the inside of her thigh. It rasped lightly against her tights. The sound sent her heart rocketing. His touch had it thumping back to earth.

She might be beyond thinking, but she wasn't beyond self-preservation. Her only hope was to dance like a partner, not a puppet. So she turned when the music ordered it and sidled up to him, back keenly arched, chest slinking along his. Her scarf was askew, her nipples taut, her leotard catching on the tear in his T-shirt. Her muscles tingled from something besides exertion, and inside her a melting began.

From now on, she vowed, she'd choreograph nothing sexier than gavottes.

He put one leg between hers. She jumped away as if burned. Then she stepped on his toes.

"No no no," he said, drawing her back with a hand on her hip. "Keep going."

A corner of her conscious mind told her they were being watched. Maybe it was the knowing smiles wherever she turned, but she had to show him who was in charge. Deliberately, she twined her arms around his neck, an embrace but an exaggeration of one at the same time. Choreographed and planned by her.

Count, she ordered herself. Six, seven, eight, turn. This was art, it wasn't real.

At least it wasn't until his arms snaked around her waist and the twinkle in his eyes turned into a dark glimmering. "May I untie you?"

He didn't wait for her consent, mistaking her consternation for concentration. In time to the music, he reached up and undid the knot in her shawl, drawing it down the front of her body.

The silk whispered like the shuffling of their feet. "Relax," he said.

She closed her eyes. It was easier than watching all the other dancers watching them, than listening to the cricketlike clatter of cameras. Easier than seeing the shape they made in the mirror.

They were a perfect blend of contrast and tension, his dark looks, sculptured face, and honed body compared to her fair hair, her pale, delicate looks, and a body that was just as honed but showed it in different ways, through control, grace, and fluidity.

In fact, Mariah had never felt quite so fluid in all her life.

Turning her back to him, she let her head roll against his shoulder and rest there as their bodies swayed. His head dipped, his lips resting on the side of her neck. A shiver rustled through her like a breeze over bare skin. The music died away.

Mariah opened her eyes. A pin could have dropped. The floor could have fallen away. The dancers didn't move.

Shelly. Mariah's heart sank as her eyes lit on the girl who danced this in performance, the one who should have been Stash's partner.

Shelly nodded shortly. "You guys were great. Don't change a thing."

Mariah swallowed hard, picked up her scarf, and drew it around her shoulders. Chin up, she watched herself tie it in the mirror. Coherent speech would have to wait.

"Mmm," she growled, retying the blasted knot. Silk was so slippery, like the careful balance within her company. Shelly was their youngest dancer. She had a world of promise and an ego as precarious as a preteen in high heels. Mariah had no intention of taking over her spot in *Rondelay*, but the explanation would have to come later.

"Did I pass?" Stash asked ingenuously.

The rest of the dancers laughed along with the press. None of them seemed to have heard the tension in his voice, although it rippled through Mariah like an electric current. She wasn't imagining it, not according to the shaking in her limbs.

"Perhaps it's time we talked about your contract."

The entire office staff for The Movement followed them down the corridor: Jerry, the accountant; Greg, the lawyer; Hannah, the office manager. Stash's own entourage wasn't far behind: press, television, public radio.

"Who are these people?" Mariah asked, masking her irritation. There was no way they'd fit in that tiny office. "I wished to discuss a business proposition with you."

"I have no objections to our being alone."

"Well, Hannah will have to stay. And Greg handles all contracts. Jerry—"

"Is necessary, too, I'm sure," Stash interrupted. "Mine, I'm afraid, are only parasites of the press."

The hangers-on chuckled, noting every word. How could the man stand it? Mariah wondered. He'd lived in this fishbowl for ten years. Squinting, she shielded her eyes as a light blinded her. A man came at her with a video camera perched on his shoulder like a boxy black vulture.

"They are doing a film on me. PBS. Next spring," Stash explained.

"To go with PBS last fall? *The Nutcracker* the year before that? The network special, *Stash: Brash, Flash, and Dash*?"

"You've researched me. Perhaps you and Mr. Documentary would like to compare notes."

"Do you really want to join The Movement?"

"Sounds like joining the underground, no?" He was playing to the crowd.

"This is one underground that wants to be noticed," Mariah responded just as quickly.

She opened the door to her office. "Perhaps we could limit this meeting to immediate family?" That meant Jerry, Hannah, and Greg on her side. To her surprise, Stash entered alone and shut the door.

Taking her place behind the desk, Mariah suddenly wished she'd worn a suit, something classy and slim like Hannah's, a big black jacket with shoulder pads out to there. Something that didn't cling, constantly reminding her there was a body pushing against it, stimulated and still vibrating from the music, from dancing with Stash. "Let's discuss my company."

She caught again the twinkle in his eye. "I like your company very much."

All right. If that was the way he wanted to play it, she'd be honest. "I'm ambitious, Stash. I want to accomplish things with this company, change a few stereotypes about dancers. We're noted for our maverick image."

"And I'm not?"

She'd heard of his run-ins with management, his bull-headedness and fire. But she wouldn't have been a choreographer for long if she couldn't handle a little artistic temperament. "Why do you want to join?"

"I was ready for a change." Stash's knee twinged along with his conscience. His need for change extended to more than switching dancing partners. "I want to be challenged, I want things demanded of me that haven't been."

"Working for me would be demanding. Some

men have trouble taking instruction from a woman."

"Some men haven't spent their lives learning to appreciate disciplined, dedicated, and beautiful women."

She nodded at the compliment.

"I want to be used. Use me, Mariah."

It was her turn to feel a pang of conscience; it was exactly what she'd been planning, using his name and fame to promote The Movement. Visions of "using" him as a man didn't bear thinking about, not under these circumstances. "I don't know if I'd put it that way," she demurred.

"Why not? I've been used all my life, as an example in Russia, as a defector in America, as a box office star. That's life. We use each other."

It could have sounded cold-blooded if it weren't for the way he looked at her as he stepped behind the chairs her staff were seated in.

Mariah flushed, knowing no one else caught that look. Again he had her feeling as if they were the only two in the cramped room. "You want to use me as well," she replied slowly.

"I meant only that this is life, men and women do things together. In dance, we call it partnering. I wish you to partner me. We join together."

And she was free to interpret those words any way she wanted, she realized. Mariah glanced at Hannah and Jerry for help. Not a peep. This was strictly between her and Stash.

The silence stretched like the Lycra hugging her body. Stash shrugged, put his hand on the doorknob, and Mariah watched her biggest chance for success open the door to leave.

"If you have doubts about me—"

She ordered her legs to stand. "Stash, I didn't mean to be rude. Maybe we could discuss this further."

"Then I ask only one favor."

"Yes?"

"Talk to me alone."

Before Mariah could answer, the others were on their feet. They knew a command when they heard one, even a softly spoken one. As they filed out, Mariah had the illogical sensation they were taking all the breathable air with them.

Three

The door closed, shutting out the murmur in the hallway, the tinkle of music from the rehearsal room, Constanza's voice as she conducted class. Stash turned.

"Do you want me or not?"

If only he knew. The part of Mariah that quivered like an antenna whenever he was near suspected he already did. "I believed, I hoped I could keep The Movement going on my own."

"With me you *know* you can. That's what you want, isn't it?"

Mariah's heart twinged. The man was playing her like a fiddle, and her body felt the vibrations. Blunt honesty might be best. "It's you and me I'm unsure of."

"So I guessed."

She unclenched her fist once more and decided halfway there not to cross her arms again. "You leave NBT and announce you're joining us the same night. Isn't that rather sudden?"

He shrugged. "A person knows when he's unhappy. He searches and searches until the right moment, and when it comes, he goes. Defecting is no time to second-guess yourself."

Mariah wondered if that applied to his relationships—if you're unhappy, leave and don't look back. "But why us? There are a dozen other companies."

He walked around the side of the desk she was hiding behind and sat on the edge. This time his foot was clad in a soft dancing shoe. It was the only soft thing about him. "I like your style."

"Mine or my company's?"

"Both. But I see you're not happy with that answer."

"I don't come with the contract, Stash."

He shrugged, continental, sophisticated, and, she suspected, miles ahead of her in this kind of game.

"Why us?" she asked again. "I need to know."

Stash was looking at the answer. It had large brown eyes, a face like porcelain, and a delicacy that belied her physical strength. Five minutes earlier he'd been holding that answer, drawn to the emotional honesty that radiated from her. So different from his own experience, growing up in a world where opinions and emotions were closely guarded, dangerous things.

But was this any safer? he asked himself. The depth of his need for her shook him, more surprising than the physical attraction. Watching the flush on her cheeks, the fire in her eyes, the attraction was easily explained. But not easy to admit. Not if he wished to soothe her suspicions about his intentions.

"I wish to keep dancing," he said. "Your style is different from the classical dance I've done. Not so much jumping or heavy lifting." He smiled in a self-deprecating way. "Your women dance side by side with the men. I like that very much. And the emotion . . ." His voice trailed off. The emotion was very nearly everything.

Mariah drew a shallow breath, aware there were things he wasn't saying, warnings she wasn't heeding. "Learning a new style isn't easy."

He took her hand in his. "Each time is new." And love itself, if it happened, would be entirely new.

When he touched his lips to the back of her hand, she shrank back subtly. Curious, he mused. The emotion he craved, she seemed to fear. Very well then. Let her think of him as a man who'd left Russia for nothing more than money, women, and fame. She was the choreographer. He'd let her set the pace, show him the kind of moves he had to make.

"I'm not promising I'll dance with you," she said.

"A shame, but I suspect I'll live."

He conceded the point, sitting on the edge of the desk as nonchalantly as a man waiting for a train, his foot tapping in time to the far off music. Mariah, on the other hand, felt like a dancer who'd completely lost the beat. Worst of all, she had no idea what to do with her hands, especially the one that still hummed from the touch of his lips.

"We can't pay you what you're worth."

"Give me a stage, music, and dances to dance. I'll be happy."

"That's it?" She barely kept the distrust out of her voice.

No, that wasn't it, Stash knew, not by any

means. But everything else would have to wait until he figured out his next move. "That's it."

She looked doubtful.

"I apologize for giving you the wrong impression," he added. "My English is, how do you say it, poor?"

She knew right then his English was, how do you say it, perfectly fine.

"I get confused between words and actions. I see the body as something to be used, and the most beautiful movement of all is between a man and a woman. Don't you agree?"

She nodded slowly. Yes, she used bodies to create beauty, to express emotions. But her emotions around Stash were too complex. Though they'd finished dancing more than twenty minutes before, she could still feel his body aligned with hers. She didn't get more vulnerable than that.

He was warming to the subject, though, and it was clear he cared deeply. She almost suspected he'd guessed the quickest way to her heart . . . and was milking it for all he was worth.

"The bodies you use are all different, not robots like some choreographers have. I may look like a classical dancer, but I want freedom."

"Freedom."

"Dancing gave me my freedom, politically. Now I look for freedom in dance. Emotional freedom. Passion."

Passion. Mariah took a deep breath, aware she was agreeing to something that was beyond contracts, something they'd never sign in black and white. How could she ask him not to seduce her? How could she promise not to succumb? Was there a clause in any contract on the planet that covered feelings like these? "You'll join us, then."

"Thank you," he replied gravely. "You've made my life worth living."

She laughed with a little puff of breath. "I wouldn't go that far."

"I would, Mariah."

She should have seen it coming. She did. Yet nothing prepared her for it. He kissed her left cheek, her right. When she turned her head to present him with the left again, he pressed one finger to her chin and stopped her, slowly bringing her face to his.

He paused, studying her lips as carefully as she studied the shadows his lashes made, black and spiky, as dark as the pupils of the eyes staring at her. A woman could get lost in those eyes, or in a kiss like the one that followed.

Their lips touched; he didn't open his mouth. He lingered, pressing, making no mistake about his intentions. His breath was soft on her skin, a sigh, an exhalation. The tip of his tongue touched her upper lip, the merest outline.

She couldn't have said later when her mouth opened, or why. Why her breasts ached to be pressed to his chest, or why her body pleaded to be held against that taut strength. She had no answers, except that fantasy was no longer enough, she had to taste him. One taste. She opened her mouth.

"Mariah."

She loved the way that felt, his lips on hers, the sound of her name in her mouth, the way his tongue filled her, thick against hers one moment, touching her teeth with its tip the next. She couldn't remember how long it had been since she'd felt such abandon build in her, so many sensations shudder through her.

"Isolate." The word whispered through her mind. "Concentrate." The only thing she could concentrate on was one isolated movement, the single sensation of his lips brushing hers, once, twice, gently, urgently, then gone.

Stash lifted his mouth from hers. He peered over her shoulder at the wall, feeling the burn in his lungs, his lower body. He might have just run a race, he might have leaped off a cliff. Did it matter? He was committed; there was no going back. He kissed her again.

It was like dancing, he thought dimly, a movement repeated, a gesture filled with meaning but never fully explained. How could you explain finding in a woman you barely knew so much of what had seemed to be missing? It was elemental, like chemistry, like lightning, a body-aching need to connect.

Reassurance wasn't something he often needed. He wanted it now. "Is our contract sealed, Mariah?"

Her eyes fluttered open. "Contract?"

All the air rushed out of her lungs. She had to drag it back in by force as she pulled herself away from him and rifled through papers on her desk. She was tumbling head over heels and he still had the presence of mind to think of contracts. That ought to tell her something. Oh, Mariah!

"There's a contract here somewhere," she muttered. Not that she'd recognize it if she found it. Every paper on her desk seemed written in Chinese, or Russian. She couldn't have read a stop sign right then, although stopping was exactly what she must do, she told herself.

"Let me lay down some rules." She said them quickly, before her nerve failed. "One: I run this company."

He nodded as she grasped a handful of pens and pencils and stuffed them in a cup.

"Two: I decide who dances with whom and when and which roles."

He slid open the center drawer of her desk, just brushing the tops of her thighs with it as she rapidly dumped in a handful of file folders. He got his fingers out before she slammed it shut again.

"Three: Shelly will probably be your partner. She's seventeen, Stash."

She looked directly at him for the first time since he'd kissed her. Stash didn't like the doubts he saw in her eyes, but he knew whom to blame. He'd ruined his only chance to play chaste and chivalrous by making it plain how much he wanted her. "Seventeen," he repeated. "And that means?"

"You don't pull this charming-star routine with her."

"You think that's what I'm doing?"

"She's very vulnerable right now, it's a bad age. Her body is just—Her dancing is at a point—Her confidence—"

"Hormones."

"Yes, but I'd appreciate it if you didn't use that word around her. She has some growing up to do, and she'll do it best without romantic interference."

"You call what we were doing interference?"

Mariah resisted the pull of his voice, the way his eyes guarded against hurt. Her own emotions might be reduced to overcooked spaghetti around him, but Shelly was more delicate and Mariah felt responsible. She knew all too well the insecurities and fears of a young dancer, how easy it would be to fall in love with someone like Stash. Why, all a girl would have to do was dance with him—

She planted her feet firmly on the ground, holding a sheaf of papers in front of her like a shield. "Unfortunately, The Movement isn't one of those companies with a large chorus. Shelly doesn't have a group of other girls to learn from, peers who've seen more of life than she has. She's on her own."

"And you've taken her under your wing."

"So to speak."

"Mariah."

He touched her shoulder. She kept the quaking to herself.

"I'll be gentle," he promised softly. Humor flashed in his eyes.

A thread snapped. Mariah called it temper. "Four: I don't like sarcasm."

He tilted his head to the side. "What do you like?"

"For you not to sit on the edge of my desk, if you please."

"Certainly. Is there anything else you like? Making love in the afternoon? Taking long baths?"

She glared at him.

"With a lover or without?" he added.

It was a game to him, she thought, and she'd been too gauche to realize it. "Go ahead, tease all you like." If she acted immune, she'd be immune. Wasn't that the way it worked?

"What about wine?"

"What about it?"

"Do you drink it from a glass or a lover's mouth?"

She slapped the folder onto the desk and shoved a drawer shut with a cock of her hip. "I'll have the contracts drawn for you." Like swords.

"I'll sign them."

"Good."

She turned abruptly away from him. This agreement wouldn't be sealed with a kiss.

Instead, he touched the back of her neck, his look of concern hidden from her. "How can you teach class when you're this tense?"

She gripped a piece of paper in her hand, striving for control. "I've got a lot to think about. This grant, for instance. Without it, I doubt we'd make it through the summer."

"Surely my joining will help."

She stopped cold. For the last few minutes she'd been so busy warding off his attraction, she'd forgotten the real benefits of his joining. "Yes, it will, won't it?" The publicity was locked in. Already they were fielding calls left and right about season tickets. Funding wouldn't be far behind. The grant form, completed the previous week, might not even be necessary.

Without realizing it, she began planning aloud. "We could hire a full-time assistant for Hannah, pay our office volunteers. You know, with all the extra help, I might even find time to dance!" The words were out before she could catch them.

Stash simply smiled. She couldn't dim the light in her eyes. The woman wanted to dance. And he wanted very badly to dance with her. "Save some of that time to teach me," he said, retying the sweater draped around his shoulders.

As he moved, Mariah caught the light scent of

sweat. She remembered the way his chest glistened in the studio, and didn't like remembering. "It may not be much fun, learning to dance again. You'll be a raw beginner."

He laughed a low and throaty laugh, then chucked her under the chin. "Lovely lady, I haven't been raw since I was thirteen. Relax." He punctuated his command with a light pat on her behind.

Mariah's eyes flared as he sauntered out the door. The crowd in the hallway stopped her on the threshold, or she would have marched after him and given him a piece of her mind. Instead, she could only gape as he turned, grinned at her, and proceeded backward down the corridor, flapping his elbows like a chicken. "Loosen up, lady dancer! You can't move if you're tight like that."

She stepped back into her office and slammed the door. Part of her hoped and prayed he'd turn around before he tumbled down the stairs. The other part simmered with fury. She could feel the flames in her cheeks, not to mention the handprint on her other cheek. Even worse, her neck and shoulders were knotted enough to start a headache.

She strode back to her desk, grant request crumpled in her hand. Absentmindedly, she lifted her elbows and flapped them, laughing in spite of herself. He was unpredictable, volatile, egotistical, and charming. He kissed like a man who loved to kiss. And she'd managed somehow not to hurl herself at him body and soul. That had to count for something.

She'd have to dance with him, in the studio if not onstage, touching him, coaching him. Yes, she was thrilled, but it wasn't the right kind of thrilled.

The sexual component was all wrong. Or was it? Wasn't sexuality part of any star's power? Maybe it was simply normal to react to it.

Mariah roughly flipped open a manila folder and stuck the grant form inside. Self-control was a small price to pay for snaring a dancer any other choreographer in the U.S. would kill for. Now all she had to do was avoid being captured in return.

Stash concentrated on his stretching while Mariah took the women through a series of moves. Shelly was indeed a beauty, willowy and a shade gawky. She could dance the parts, but hadn't yet earned the emotion or confidence Mariah invested them with.

"Be yourself," Mariah coaxed.

"How?" Shelly wailed.

"Dance what you're feeling."

"But what am I supposed to be feeling?"

Mariah gave her a quick hug. "You'll learn."

Watching them, Stash knew exactly what *he* felt. Not showing it was his problem. He caught Mariah's eye; she looked away. He hung back with the male dancers and let another fifteen minutes drag by.

Given the chance, he'd show her emotion. He'd dance until her blood burned in her veins. But she was busy with other dancers. She'd deftly avoided him for two weeks. He told himself he didn't need to be the center of attention just because he was a star. But dammit, she was the center of his attention.

As Danny, their other primary male dancer, demonstrated a series of steps for the men, Stash forced his thoughts back to work. Imitating, learning, anticipating, itching to show off. Given half a chance, he'd steal Mariah's breath away.

"Take a break, ladies."

As Mariah turned her attention to the men, Stash stood front and center, ready to dance, ready to burst.

"Danny," she said, "would you demonstrate *Cocteau Cocktail* for us?"

Stash watched, fierce concentration darkening his eyes.

Mariah nodded, smiling, when Danny finished. "Now Bill?"

Bill, another regular, was slightly stiffer, less exuberant. Not Mariah, Stash noticed. She crouched in front of the wall of mirrors, balancing on her toes, her hands clasped loosely between her knees. He watched the way her eyebrows danced, up and down, matching the corners of her mouth when she smiled in delight at the comic number. Her fingers moved, her wrist loose as she signaled a pirouette, her palm open for a long, slow gesture. She laughed out loud at one point, and Stash's stomach tightened. Then she caught his gaze and he suspected her stomach tightened just as his had.

Standing, she wiped her palm down her thigh and tugged at the form-fitting stretch pants she wore. "All right, Stash. I know this is new for you."

"Try me." It was an order. A plea.

"*Cocktail* or something you know?"

"I may know this."

He'd seen it danced only twice, but Mariah let that pass. "Give it a shot."

He did, and came in too early.

Mariah waved to Janine. "From the top."

He was early again. Mariah had to step in, dashing the niggling hope that somehow he'd have picked everything up by osmosis.

She demonstrated. At her side, he followed. Once he put his hand on her hip. Another time he touched her arm. Always he was professional. He instinctively tuned in to the humor, the dips, the Charlie Chaplin tilt of the head. In fifteen minutes he looked like a Movement dancer. In half an hour Mariah had almost convinced herself they could work together like adults.

Then he stripped off his T-shirt and said, "From the top."

This time there was no hesitating. He didn't need her guidance. He danced the part with assurance and style, leading inexorably to the final breathtaking leap. Everyone in the room seemed to hold his breath until Stash touched down again, front knee bent, rear leg extended behind him in a lunge. Everyone was watching him fly. Mariah was watching him flinch.

Before she could open her mouth to ask if he was all right, he was on his feet. "Okay?" He tossed the hair off his forehead, the look in his eyes fierce with denied pain.

"Fine," she murmured. She knew in that instant he'd never admit weakness. And he knew she'd seen it. She wondered if he'd forgive her for that. "Want to sit the next one out?"

"No rest for the wicked."

Everyone else laughed.

"It was good, no?" Stash waved his T-shirt off-handedly before putting it on, his eyes burning into hers, daring her to say otherwise. It was obvious he'd thoroughly impressed everyone except the woman who was supposed to be.

Ego, Mariah thought. It was as good a shield as any. But pop psychology was little comfort. Her star was dancing hurt. A tiny curl of fear ran through her. What had she gotten herself and her company into?

Four

Mariah was hot on Stash's heels as he left the building. "Stash!"

Unfortunately, a dozen reporters were trailing those same million-dollar heels.

"Can we have a quote, Stash?"

"How's class?"

"Are the rumors true about you and—"

He swung around, his leather coat slung over his shoulders like a cape. "Maybe later, fellows. Thanks."

Mariah ducked under the arm he waved them away with. "Got a few minutes for me?"

He smiled as if he couldn't believe his luck. Then he lowered his arm and settled it familiarly around her shoulders. "For you, darling, a lifetime."

Darlink, she thought. And the "just pals" embrace. And the paparazzi snapping away. "I need to talk to you."

"Shall we say my place?"

His forwardness didn't faze her. She knew he

was beginning to learn he could tease her—and taking much pleasure in it. The fact that half these people were writing it down only added to her irritation.

"How about we walk?" she suggested.

He loped along with her as if walking were his favorite pastime, as if having his arm around her made the world a wonderful place. "You don't mind our entourage?"

"I can't say I'm getting used to them," Mariah admitted.

"They want us to do something photograph-able."

Judging from the clicking, she thought, Stash taking a walk was news.

A photographer jogged ahead, training his camera on them. "Give us a kiss," he taunted.

Mariah almost gave him something else.

"Not a good idea," Stash cooed in her ear, clutching her closer to his side.

She didn't know which bothered her more, that the cameraman had gotten a shot of Stash nuzzling her ear or the tingling it caused up and down her skin. "Oh, for Pete's sake, he was only talking to me," she snapped.

"Wait'll you see the picture. Any truth to the rumors?"

"I know a restaurant," Stash murmured. "We could sneak in."

Before the "Please, let's" was out of her mouth, Stash was ducking her down an alley, running full speed past garbage cans and through the narrow clearing between a brick wall and a truck unloading crates of lettuce. Mariah glimpsed another street at the end, but Stash wasn't going through.

Just past the truck he pulled her up short and ushered her through a blank metal door.

They stood chest to chest in the blackness, listening to the running feet and shouted curses outside, their labored breathing inside. She might be in fine shape, but his burst of speed had winded her. He could have been a sprinter if he hadn't been a dancer. She chuckled. A finger touched her lips and her heart leaped.

"Shh," he said soothingly.

Pounding crazily, her heart didn't get the message. She'd thought for a moment he'd been about to kiss her.

Her nose adjusted faster than her eyes, and Mariah picked up mouth-watering smells. "Is this the restaurant?"

"The best. I often sneak out the back, but I've never come in this way. We'll go through the kitchen."

The kitchen was a stab of white light in between the hall and the gloomy restaurant. Except for the candle on each table, the booths were heavily shadowed. When they sat, Stash reached across the table and covered her hand with his. "You wanted to be alone with me?"

"In a sense, yes," she said hesitantly. She wasn't the starstruck teenager she had been. She had experience, some élan, or so she hoped. She simply hadn't figured out where it all disappeared to when Stash gazed at her across a wavering candle, his eyes dark, his smile slow and wide. She got down to business. "It's about this afternoon."

"Ah." He leaned back, receding into darkness that matched his eyes and ebony hair. "I'm sorry about the paparazzi." He shrugged as if apologizing for something he had no control over, the weather, the traffic.

"You encourage them."

He shrugged again, this time knowingly. "It's a game. They enjoy, I enjoy."

"I don't. Not when I'm the pawn."

"If it makes you feel that way, I'll change."

"I meant, you're letting them believe we're having an affair."

"We're not."

"I know that."

"And your dancers?"

"They know that. The only time we're together, we're in public. Nothing's going on."

"I know."

Darkness should increase a person's ability to listen, Mariah thought. So why couldn't she decide if that was regret in his voice or resignation? "Why are you feeding the rumors? You never deny them."

"I'm superstitious that way. Saying there's nothing may lead to nothing."

She let out a frustrated sigh. "People are going to think you joined The Movement because we're lovers. You and this 'little known New York dance troupe,' to quote the latest tabloid."

"But as you say, they can't prove it since we are never alone. Except now." He touched her hand. "Why do you fear this?"

"I don't."

"Then hold my hand and say it. Look into my eyes and deny it."

She did just that. "We're not lovers."

"And never will be?"

Her stomach felt hollow, her nerves as scoured

and raw as the unpainted brick wall beside her. "You want total honesty?"

His grip on her hand demanded it.

"Tell me about the knee, Stash."

He glanced around as if he could actually see in the inky darkness. A waiter appeared at their table seconds later. "Let me order you a drink. Do you drink alcohol?"

"Not much."

"Then white wine."

The waiter faded away. Mariah felt exhaustion steal over her. This could very well be the first time she'd sat all week. Articles, interview requests, attention, offers. On no more than the assurance that she could type and speak English, Mariah had hired an assistant to field the calls and take ticket requests. And she'd acquired a world-class star who was dancing hurt.

"The knee, Stash. Dancing, like love, requires emotional honesty."

"I haven't lied to you."

"Haven't you?" The very idea caused pain, and that surprised her. "Then tell me the problem."

"I've danced since I was nine. A body can only take so much."

"And yours?"

"In a wonderful American phrase, it has its days."

"Stash."

"All right." He looked at her straight, eyes black and icy and guarded. Eyes like that could stare down the KGB, she thought. And probably had. "Some tendinitis," he said, "possibly calcium deposits."

"And? Stash, I don't want to interrogate you."

"Don't worry. People more expert than you have tried."

She fought off a shudder and a wave of sympathy, but he wasn't asking for pity.

"The legs are always the first to go," he added. "That is another popular expression, yes?"

"Not when they're your legs. Can you dance?"

His fist curled around a crumpled linen napkin. "I have to dance."

Again Mariah felt a wave of sympathy, and more. Empathy. She might know nothing more about Russia than what she'd read in spy novels, but when it came to what a dancer felt about facing the end of a career . . . "I know exactly how you feel."

"Do you?" He didn't challenge, merely asked.

"I went through it myself. The fear, the questioning. Being a dancer becomes a person's whole identity. To see the end of the line . . ."

"But you still dance. And you were willing to give it up for business reasons. Busy-ness," he reiterated caustically.

"I was willing to give it up for the second half of my life. When the dancing's over I'll have choreography."

"But for now you will dance."

She found herself promising him she would. "For this season."

"So it's not really over."

"It was. When I was fifteen. I grew too fast."

He shrugged as if that happened to everyone.

She made a face and, with a wave of her hand, indicated her chest. "In all the wrong places. Your body may be wearing out, but mine didn't give me a chance. I got gawky and self-conscious and hysterical and depressed. I bought bras that were too small and dieted like mad, thinking that would make a difference."

She paused as the waiter set down their drinks, then held on to her glass with both hands, studying the wine. "I even considered surgery." It was hard to convey the feelings that cut through her as she admitted it.

"So have I," he replied softly.

"But you're talking about an injury. Why should a perfectly healthy girl, a young woman, have to mutilate her body just to dance? To live up to some ideal of what a dancer is supposed to look like?" The words tumbled out. "I was so ashamed of becoming a woman."

The candle sputtered in the silence.

"You didn't have the surgery," he said quietly.

It took her a moment to put into words the shame she'd never revealed to anyone. "I did see a surgeon. A friend took me. I raided my college fund for the money. But I couldn't go through with it. I quit dancing that very day."

"And?"

This part was easier; she'd explained it in numerous interviews. Having Stash listening made it more personal, though, more cleansing. She needed him to understand, even if she wasn't sure why. Some kind of connection was being made. Not touching, not dancing, but connecting all the same.

"I got through my final year of high school, desperately making up for all the childhood I'd supposedly missed by dedicating myself to dance. Then, after a couple years of being miserable in college, I got roped into the cheerleading squad. No, go ahead, laugh."

He crooked a smile.

"Next thing I know I'm choreographing routines. Then the theater department does *Oklahoma!* and needs someone to block out the ballet."

"And you were a choreographer."

"Not quite that fast, but I saw a light. I thought, if I can come up with a style of modern dance, a style I'd never considered before, then I could dance. Other people have done it."

But very few women like Mariah Heath, Stash thought. It was clear the memories were painful, but her eyes were alight now with a tale of discovery.

"I realized I could dance again! And make a place for other people like me. Not"—she held out a hand as if stopping his thoughts right there—"not a company of big-breasted beauties, mind you."

He laughed out loud.

"No, a company of dancers who, for one reason or another, don't fit the mold. People who dance for the love of it, the emotion. There's so much more to it than steps."

He nodded, watching the love, the passion, flickering across her face. He wanted to take her in his arms right then. No one this giving, this caring, should ever have been ashamed of being a woman. He knew he could show her its joys.

"But I'm rambling," she said, sensing his mind was wandering. "Giving you my 'reason for being' speech. I'm sorry."

"No, I liked it. Maybe I am another . . . what do you call them, lame duck? . . . you can use for your company."

She grimaced and lowered her voice. "About the

knee. I'd be a complete hypocrite if I suggested you hurt yourself more to go on dancing."

"Are you thinking of firing me?"

She gasped and choked on the wine. The heat of the alcohol flushed her cheeks. "After what I went through to hire you?"

"Was it that hard?"

He'd never know the emotional wringer she sometimes went through merely looking at him, catching him watching her in rehearsal, reliving the kiss in her office. Fearing, and hoping, it would happen again. "I've had more interviews in three weeks than I had in three years. I'm about talked out, and here you are getting me to talk more. Now, about you."

"I know my body."

"Do you want me to program easier numbers for you?"

"No!" He quickly lowered his voice, the black gaze fastened on her. "I will not be babied and I won't ask you to compromise your work."

"Part of my method is to treat my dancers as individuals. I play to their strengths. I want to work this out between us."

He reached across the table, his fingertips touching the soft skin of her cheek. He felt the quickening pulse along the side of her neck. "I want it to work too, Mariah."

A searing flash of lightning cut through the darkness, blinding her. "Oh, my God!"

"One more. Hold it there," the photographer commanded.

Mariah's string of curses flew by so fast, Stash could barely pick out the ones that were new to him.

"Out! Out!" He swung his coat like a matador's cape, knocking the camera out of the man's hands.

As the man scooped it up, Stash and Mariah stalked out of the restaurant.

"I hate this!" Mariah yelled. "Everywhere we turn!"

"It's only more rumors."

"That's not a rumor, it's a front-page photo! How do you live like this?"

"This is fame. You wanted it too."

"Not like this. And you, if I may say so, haven't been much help."

"Slow down. My English still isn't good."

"Well, it's good enough for them."

"I've tried to keep the spotlight on your company."

"And all they want to hear is if *we're* keeping company!"

"If you want a private life, you shouldn't dance in public."

Marching down the evening streets, she considered his words, her lips twisting in a sardonic smile. *Private life.* She'd never feared losing hers because she didn't really have one. Evenings spent curled up on the sofa drinking hot chocolate and watching *Larry King Live*, weren't going to be covered by the eleven o'clock news.

Picturing tomorrow's headlines, though, she stopped in the middle of the sidewalk and whirled on him. "This has got to stop. There has to be a way to keep them out."

"It's a public restaurant."

"I mean from rehearsals. What if someone else had noticed your flinching today?"

She was close enough to the truth to make him wince again. Still, he shook his head so forcefully that an errant lock of hair fell over his forehead once more. "If you bar them, they'll say I'm injured."

"I'll deny it."

"They'll believe it even more." His logic was skewed, but she knew he had a point.

"So what do we do? Do I play witch and simply kick everyone out because I'm in charge?"

"I'm sure you'll think of something, boss lady."

Mariah sighed. "It's not only the press, it's everything. Those Russian refugees who come around asking for money you never deny them, the clothing manufacturers' reps licensing your name on that line of exercise wear, the movie producers, the lawyers . . . all of it's distracting."

"Those are investments to support me when my legs can't."

"But it's dangerous, don't you see? If any of them saw you flinch today, it'd be all over the papers. We've got to be alone."

He couldn't argue with her there. "Name the time and place, Mariah."

She startled him by doing so. "Interlochen, Michigan."

It didn't take Stash long to find out where Interlochen was. A summer camp for gifted young people from all over the world, it was a world away from New York City. Mariah explained it at the next class, this one closed to the press.

"I've been invited to teach for an eight-week term, June and July, at a summer camp. I can't take all of you with me, but I want us to keep working, especially on the solo numbers. My plan is this. Stash, you have to come because you have a lot to learn. Since they have to give you a cabin, they'll let Danny bunk with you. Shelly, I want you there as well. You can bunk with me."

"Bunk?" Shelly squeaked. "What kind of camp is this?"

"They're cottages. Log cabins, I think."

"Do they have plumbing?" the girl asked dubiously.

"I'm sure they do."

"I won't have to make wallets, will I?"

"You may well be the most accomplished young dancer there. I'd like your help in the master classes I'm going to be teaching. Your experience as a professional will be an example to the girls."

Shelly stood up straighter, and Mariah breathed a sigh of relief. Being the oldest instead of the youngest might do a lot for Shelly's ego, not to mention her confidence. Responsibility was a good road to maturity.

"Danny," she went on, "you're coming to help Stash learn the male leads. Everybody else, this doesn't mean I'm letting you go. I want you to continue working with Constanza in class. Now that we've got her on the payroll, we're going to use her to the fullest. I'll be back in August and we'll have one month, one intense month, to go over the ensemble pieces in time for the September premier. Is that okay with you?"

The dancers were in little position to object, and Mariah was thankful that grousing was minimal.

"All right, then, our new assistant"—she blanked out on the name—"uh . . . Dorothy is going to see to the plane tickets. Everyone else report to class as usual."

It was an unorthodox move, but it would get her much-needed private time to tutor Stash. This overlit goldfish bowl was no place to work. Closing the door to her office, Mariah looked down at the tabloid page still crumpled in her hand, aware she'd carried it into and out of the rehearsal room. She groaned and wadded it tighter.

She didn't need to see the half-page photo to remember the way that man and woman had been caught looking at each other across a candle, his fingertips lightly caressing her face.

The paper hit the rim of the wastebasket with a reverberating clang.

The last day of May. Mariah took a deep breath and watched the tree trunks flicker by as the van pulled up to the summer camp entrance. "We're here," the driver called.

It definitely wasn't New York. The tallest things were the pines sheltering dark brown cottages. The rustic cabins alternated with brick buildings. From each one, music issued forth.

She saw groups of students walking the paths as the van angled into a parking space. Instrument cases brushed the navy corduroy slacks of camp uniforms. Light blue shirts adorned with pins, scarves, and other additions individualized the look. The combination of teenagers and creativity saw to it that uniforms weren't uniform for long.

Their luggage stacked on a rolling cart, Mariah's small group followed a guide down the asphalt path.

"Fifty paces and I've counted thirteen violins, three cellos, and a piano in every doorway," Danny commented in his slow Texas drawl.

Mariah nodded, not mentioning how many heads she'd counted turning at the sight of Stash-kolnikov. Or the boys who'd noticed Shelly.

Dressed in severe New Yorker black, Shelly graciously ignored them. "Is it mostly music?"

"Most of the students are here for that," their guide said. "We also have acting, some writing, and dance. You'll meet the rest of the faculty at lunch tomorrow. I'm afraid evenings are pretty full with performances. We like to emphasize experience as much as practice."

"Where's the rehearsal hall?" Mariah asked.

He pointed out a dark wood building at the foot of a hill next to an outdoor amphitheater. "The orchestra practices there."

"Something to dance to besides piano," Stash joked.

"I'll give you a copy of their rehearsal schedule too."

"Thanks," Mariah said.

"Here's your cabin, ladies."

"Like it?" Mariah asked Shelly as they settled in, scanning the pine-paneled walls, twin beds, and small kitchenette.

"It looks okay," the teenager replied, her worldly air firmly in place.

"You haven't checked out the bathroom."

"I need at least an hour in the morning," Shelly stated quickly, staking out her territory.

Mariah smiled. "It's all yours."

"This place reminds me of Russia," Stash said, peering in their screen door.

"Come on in."

Shelly glanced up at the brightening in Mariah's voice. Mariah toned it down. "Unpacked already?"

"Yes. Danny's gone looking for a cigarette machine."

Mariah clucked in disapproval. "Doubt he'll find one here." She peeked out the window at the small knot of students hovering at the end of their row of cabins. "Do entourages form everywhere you go?"

"Dance students. Word got around you were bringing more than your expertise."

"I'll bet it did." She noticed Shelly, perched on the bed, glancing out the corner of her eye at the students. "Why don't you go and introduce yourself?"

Shelly took her time unfolding her long legs. "Might as well," she said and sauntered out.

Mariah rolled her eyes as the screen door slammed. "No MTV. That's worse than no plumbing."

Stash smiled, watching the introductions outside. "She'll be busy enough. A couple of those young men—"

"Don't you even think it!"

"When I was that age, that's all I thought of."

"Why am I not surprised?" Mariah flopped unceremoniously onto her bed, uncomfortably aware of his gaze on her.

He came over and sat down near her feet. "There's life beyond dancing, Mariah. Isn't that a lesson we all need to learn at some point?"

He'd learned later than he should have, he added silently, after too many affairs, too many light-hearted, empty-headed romances. He was tired of games, of always keeping what mattered most hidden inside.

That was why he'd prized the past two weeks in New York. Mariah had danced with him, surprising him, letting him closer than he'd expected, calling on him to express emotions he rarely showed. That was only when they danced, though. Outside the rehearsal room she'd been as busy with her burgeoning dance company as he'd been with his business ventures.

The music camp was a chance to escape all that.

And yet, any hope he'd harbored of having Mariah to himself had been dashed that morning on the plane when she handed him their rehearsal schedule. Her teaching schedule was on the back. They'd have time to work, but little time alone. He wondered if she'd planned it that way.

Smiling as he thought of how he'd get around that schedule, he touched her leg.

Mariah sat up so fast, her head swam in the humid midsummer weather. "Tell me why this camp reminds you of Russia."

"We had a place like this for artists. My teacher's dacha. Only his favorite students were invited."

"He was fond of you?"

"Like a father, a hero to me. He took a homeless boy and taught him how to live."

"Homeless?"

"My mother sent me to Moscow to study. I stayed in the dormitory. That is not a real home."

Mariah tried to picture his mother. It was easier than picturing Stash as a boy. There was too much man in him, too much knowledge and skill, and maybe too much pain.

"Didn't you miss your family?" she asked gently.

He still did. But that wasn't what she meant. "I got over it by spending all my time in school, practicing and pestering Sergei to teach me more. This is why I'm good."

Loneliness and hard work. Mariah knew them well. "Probably some genetics in there too."

He shrugged, and she wondered if he was aware of the way he'd pestered her the last two weeks, working, demanding, revealing what she asked him to reveal, eager to please and getting closer all the time.

She found it nearly impossible to dance with him and not be moved, excited, stimulated. Keeping her body from registering emotion was diametrically opposed to her vision of dance. On the other hand, showing Stash the simmering emotions he evoked in her went against every shred of self-protection she'd mustered.

Entwined together, body to body, moving rhythmically to the music, she felt raw in his arms, too needy, too willing, too combustible. She needed protection, not ignition. But every time he touched her, the sparks began.

At least they'd be busy here, she thought. And safe. No tabloids to spur romantic rumors, no love affairs to deny. His hand slid from her ankle to her calf. No, no love at all, she insisted silently.

He spoke again, and his voice was soft and intimate, like the music drifting on the air outside. "When I became a big star, I brought my family to Moscow to live. I was such a hero, the successful son. My mother and sister were very impressed."

"And your father?"

"He died long before. That is why Sergei became

my father. He told me I was worth his wasting his time on. He was what you call a drill sergeant and I was needing this."

She bent her knee, gently extracting her leg from under his hand. "He must have given you a lot of encouragement."

He ran a finger over the arch of her foot, dipping into her sandal to do so.

The tremors from his touch grew harder to ignore. Her toes curled. He made a circle on her anklebone with a fingertip. It was starting all over again. Music, movement, their private dance, beginning with nothing more than his hand on her skin, her body responding, shuddering in deep, private places.

"Tell me more about Sergei," she managed to say.

The loving memories faded as Stash's eyes clouded with more recent, painful memories. "He's dead now. He was sick for many years."

"I'm sorry."

"I should have been."

"What do you mean?" It was hard to believe he could be so cold about anything that clearly meant so much to him. A chill ran through her that had nothing to do with his touch.

"I didn't go back. No visits, no funeral."

There it was again, a hint of pain, so well-hidden. Like his flinch at rehearsal, she wouldn't have noticed if she hadn't been watching so intently. "But you defected. You couldn't exactly drop in for a weekend."

He turned away and got off the bed. "I danced the premiere of *Study in G* that week. Made headlines all over the world."

"Maybe he saw them," she argued gently, "heard what you'd accomplished because of him. He might have been very proud."

"Or very bitter. The authorities accused him of helping me escape. My denying it did no good. I was a traitor and not to be believed. His position at the Bolshoi was reduced to nothing. He couldn't teach."

She began to say something, but he touched her lips lightly with his fingertips. "I'll never know, Mariah."

He bent and kissed her. Softly, no more than good-bye.

She silently bid him stay. Her hand grazed the side of his neck and she pulled him closer, her lips lightly parted, offering. "Show me, Stash," she whispered aloud, then added silently to herself, Show me what you've been hiding. Love, if it was to have a chance, required honesty.

Her body craved even more. Like a plume of smoke spiraling upward, her desire caught fire. One moment she wanted to thank him for opening up to her with words. The next, she was wrapped in sheer sensation as his mouth devoured hers, words evaporating like more smoke. Until she touched him she hadn't realized the dizzying heights to which passion could fly, as high as Stash, as immediate and daring.

He broke it off, his voice hoarse, his body taut and strained. "You've never kissed me like that." A glimmer in his eye made her think of the tenacious boy he'd been.

Her own voice was no steadier. "Are you saying you don't want me to?"

"Maybe not now."

Stash turned to the window, watching the students gathered at the end of the walk to see him. But the birches drew his attention away, the sound of music on pine-scented air, reminding him of a time before decisions about family and country had been made in an instant. In an alley in Paris, as a taxi honked its horn, a door had swung open. One irrevocable step and everything changed. As it would with Mariah if he didn't leave now.

"There is a saying in my country," he said softly. "You should know it. A man can defect from everything but his scars."

Five

The sun sat pink and hazy over the pines on the opposite side of the lake. Silence reigned at six o'clock in the morning. As Stash accustomed himself to the water lapping at his feet, he realized there was noise; it simply wasn't New York noise.

The double musical note of a bird sounded like a human whistle, a signal. Other birds twittered and cawed among the tree branches. Squirrels chased one another through the leaves and pine needles, chattering over territory. At least it wasn't photographers.

He strode out until the water was up to his knees, took a deep breath, and dove under.

He knifed through the water, then came up, gasping. It was the kind of brisk cold that took the breath away, the kind, he told himself, that would be better in ten minutes. He got to work.

It wasn't fun and it wasn't exciting, and it certainly wasn't the Bahamas, but it was better than jogging. Anything was better than jogging.

He stopped and touched bottom, the wavy ridges of sand cushioning his feet while he gauged the feel of his muscles. Absently, he swung his leg back and forth, testing the knee against the gentle resistance of the water.

Gentle resistance. The phrase described Mariah's response to him. He touched her, she wanted him. But something was in their way. He was beginning to wonder if it wasn't himself.

Cutting through the water again, he did half a dozen laps.

Mariah, he thought, gulping air, glimpsing sky. He'd come there for her. He'd made the leap and joined her company, yet part of him wasn't ready to take the final step.

He'd defected in a day and age when that meant never looking back, leaving his mother and sister behind perhaps forever. He winced at the pain, the hint of shame. Weren't ten years enough to atone for one rash, necessary act? But the situation had changed. He might be able to go back to Russia.

Mariah taught class every morning. He stood in doorways and watched. Her young female dancers looked so defenseless in black leotards and pink tights, their hair uniformly pulled back in chignons. Their arms were willows, their legs the same. They held a certain classical appeal, but none of them was a woman, none as sensual and full of life as Mariah. She demanded expression and emotion, cajoling, encouraging, giving. In return, she shared herself.

But not with him. That kiss in her cabin had scared her. His pulling away hadn't helped.

The woman had so much to give. Taking his ego

into consideration, he was convinced he was the man to love her.

The English language, so full of big words, seemed content to define an emotion this enormous with four letters. He said it out loud. "Love." Like dropping a stone in a pond, the ripples went out from there.

He loved his family and he'd left. Could he love Mariah, knowing he might have to leave her to save them? The questions beat in his veins like waves lapping the beach, one after the other, over and over.

He rolled onto his back and watched the sky lighten, reducing his kick to a small splash. His arms churned like a lazy windmill, guiding him through the water. It felt good, stretching his chest, pulling cool morning air into his hardworking lungs. He felt strong, revitalized, physical. And there was only one person he wanted to share that with.

But how could he woo her, court her, convince her, if every headline from the Soviet Union mocked his vow to jump and never look back? He was looking back now, and Mariah was there. She was part of his decision, part of his crumbling secrecy. She made him reveal so many emotions, deep, private, burning ones. As she herself said, "Movement never lied." But men did. Sometimes for good reasons.

Arcing into the water like a dolphin, he sought the colder deeper levels, someplace he could clear his head, his suddenly sluggish veins.

Mariah set down her towel and kicked off her sandals, relieved to see someone in the water. She couldn't remember if she'd ever been alone in the pool at her fitness club in New York.

"Ooooh, a cold luxury," she said, dipping her toe in the water.

"Oh, dive in," she scolded herself. "If you drown, somebody will hear you scream. It's certainly quiet enough." Holding her breath, she plunged in.

She tried not to yell bloody murder as she came up again. It was like melted ice! How could anyone swim in this? She knew she'd look like a fool running right back out, so she stayed in up to her neck, feeling her nipples tighten to painful buds as she watched her companion do another lap.

"Probably dying of hypothermia and doesn't know it," she muttered. "I'll stay in just long enough to save him."

Resting after three quick laps, she looked around. Her distant swimming companion was gone. She quickly scanned the beach. His towel was there; he wasn't.

"Damn." Her heart sank fast, exactly the way she hoped he hadn't. Setting out for deeper water, keeping her head well up in case he surfaced, she ran through what she'd learned in that lifeguard class she'd taken ten years back. "Hello," she called softly, feeling idiotic. He couldn't have drowned without so much as a splash, could he?

Her scream pierced the morning calm as an underwater body brushed her leg. Stash popped to the surface. "What the hell are you doing? You scared me half to death."

"Shh." He laughed, a finger to his lips. "You'll wake the campers."

"Stop acting like Jaws!"

"There are no sharks here."

"Don't I wish!"

He laughed at the fury in her eyes, shaking his head so that his hair flew out at angles, trailing an arc of beaded water over the surface around him. "Diving is good for lung capacity. Very aerobic."

Mariah huffed and treaded water. Stash was doing the same. Their legs bumped. She scooped her arms wide at her sides and backed up a bit, when what she really wanted was to fold those arms tightly over her chest. Although she'd forgotten all about the cold, her breasts hadn't and her plain mauve maillot wasn't very concealing.

The golden early light shone on Stash's slick hair. His lashes were even spikier when wet. Droplets of water ran off the sharp planes of his face.

Maybe she *should* cross her arms, she thought when he smiled. She'd sink like a stone, but it would be safer than having him look at her that way.

She'd gone overboard kissing him in her cabin. After two weeks the reasons and rationalizations for it were as grooved into her memory as on an old record. He'd been reaching out, sharing part of his closely held past. In return, she'd dispensed with words and tried to show him how deeply she sympathized. And idolized. And fantasized.

The results had sent her scurrying in the other direction, turning much of his tutoring of him over to Danny.

As for her melting each time they danced, he was a great dancer. It should come as no surprise that she sometimes hungered to know what kind of lover he'd be. But there were things a woman didn't risk without a lot of thought, even when desire threatened to overwhelm her like a tidal wave, or a subtle, tugging undertow.

Mariah touched the sandy bottom of the lake. Reality was keener than any early morning fantasy, and about thirty degrees colder. She'd stick with reality, thanks. "Since when do you go swimming at this hour?"

"I've been here every morning. It's better than jogging."

"How's the knee?"

He shrugged, displacing a small series of waves in her direction. "As I said, swimming is better."

"If it hurts, Stash—"

"And what brings you here?" he blithely interrupted.

Once again, he wasn't going to let her in on his pain. She sighed. "Same reason."

His look of concern was instant. "Are you hurting?"

"My chest," she said. If she had to call attention to it, better that it be under four inches of water. "Swimming is more comfortable than jogging. I just haven't gotten that many chances to be out this early."

"Ah. You've been so very busy."

"I have," she replied, fighting defensiveness and a shudder as his legs brushed hers again. She really should be tutoring him. Maybe they'd both had enough time to cool off. "Aren't you freezing yet?"

"Reminds me of Russia. I have swum in colder water than this."

And loved more beautiful women, she thought out of the blue. "I'll bet you have. But then, you always were crazy."

He looked surprised, then pleased. "You're teasing me."

There wasn't a whole lot else she could do. He was beautiful in the masculine way sculptors lived for. And he was wet, his chest covered with fine black hair, but not enough to hide the sleek skin that stretched over well-developed muscles. And the view, she knew from his dancewear and her own dreams, could only get better farther down. The rippled abdomen, the muscular thighs . . .

"But I'm interfering with your exercise," he said.

"No," she replied hurriedly. Only with her hormones.

"We'll race."

"We'll what?"

"To that floating thing, what is it?"

"A buoy."

"All right then, to buoy."

"Wait! That was a definition, not consent."

"The first there and back."

"Wins what?"

But he was already lunging into a stroke. With one deep kick he widened a four-foot lead.

"Hey!" She shushed herself. Complaining about fairness to a man with his head underwater was useless. She took off after him.

She lost by two lengths.

"Another," she demanded breathlessly. "This time I get the head start. You cheated."

"Okay."

He took off for the opposite buoy, Mariah keeping pace this time, but only at the price of burning lungs and pounding muscles. Her arms felt like noodles, her legs like cement weights. With one arm tossed around the orange and white buoy, she panted, weakly waving a hand in victory. "Beat ya' that time!"

"Then you win."

"What do I win?" The first word was saucy, the last, breathless. She might have foreseen it, might have thought of it beforehand. She most definitely should have known better.

One slow sweep of his arm underwater and Stash was body to body with her. His lips were as wet as the rest of him, parted, breath coming as hard as hers.

"Unh-uh," she said. "This water was supposed to be your cold shower for the day." She let go of the buoy to float away, but his hand was on her waist. "I take it you know the word discreet? I'm faculty here, you're a guest performer."

"And we don't want to put on a performance?"

"Not out here."

He bumped her body with his, down low, where the water was cold and she was suddenly sizzling heat.

"A shame." The word was a soft curse. He released her and swam to shore.

Walking out of the water, Mariah ground the gritty sand between her toes and shook it out of her towel. Because she'd followed at a distance, Stash was already reclining on his towel, openly watching as she patted her skin and fluffed her hair.

"Need your back done?" he asked casually. The woman needed, period, he thought. He had to find a way to show her.

She shook her head, strands of honey-red hair sprinkling him. He laughed.

Spreading her towel, she sat beside him, ignor-

ing what that laughter and his muscular chest did
to her equilibrium. She stretched her legs out,
feeling the sand sticking to the undersides of her
calves.

For all the tension he roused in her, she really
had missed talking with him. Their conversation
about his teacher had stayed with her, a tantaliz-
ing hint of the inner man. "I have been busy," she
said. "I don't want you to think I've been avoiding
you."

Stash wiped a palm over his wet hair. She had
been avoiding him, and they both knew it. Drawing his knees together, he wrapped his arms
around them and looked across the lake.

"Birches, pines, cottages, cold lakes, and short
summers," he said. "Like Russia. The smell of pine
and water."

"You've been homesick," she said, surprised but
instantly sympathetic. Shelly had been going
through the same thing, but Mariah had never
suspected Stash . . . She placed her hand lightly
on his arm.

He tensed at her touch. It was as good as pulling
away. He gave her a quick look that said he was
sorry, but that didn't negate the involuntary response.

"It's silly, you know?" he said. "Missing a place I
left deliberately. And permanently."

"You can't help how you feel."

"That's true."

"Do you ever want to go back? Some artists
have."

"Some."

But not him, his answer implied. It seemed to be

a line he'd firmly drawn, cutting him off from the past.

"They're freer now."

"Some things, Mariah, regrets, habits, are like prisons inside. They are harder to cross than borders."

"What do you mean?"

He meant secrecy and the need to protect others warring with the need to break free. Could he at last commit to someone, seize the chance to love? "Do you want to get involved with me, Mariah?"

In the soft morning quiet, his question startled her. She stuttered until he answered for her. "You don't. All right, then. We have it settled."

He stood abruptly, tugging on one of his torn T-shirts, drawing the towel around his neck, wet ends of hair dripping down the side of his neck. He was leaving.

"Pardon me," she said, "but I can answer these questions on my own."

He studied her for a long moment. "Mariah."

"What?" She sounded huffy and didn't like it. "That's just a very blunt question—do I want to get involved."

"You need it spelled out?"

"I'm a grown woman. I know what involvement means."

Did she? Stash wondered if she knew exactly how deep he meant the commitment to go. He wasn't aware of taking her hand, but when he looked down it was resting in his palm, turned over like a precious shell on the beach.

How many beaches and shells had he left behind him? Could he risk leaving another?

He looked across the lake, his gaze hardening.

"You may be right not to want me. You don't know me."

"Don't I?" She knew the way his beard grew overnight. She could practically feel it, hear the way it would rasp if she touched it. "We have some time to learn. It isn't all animal attraction, you know. Sometimes you move very fast."

He laughed shortly. "Like lightning." She'd hit him that way, but she hadn't been attracted to him as swiftly. He could accept it if he worked on it. "Isn't it easier that way? Jump and don't look back?"

"It's quicker."

He looked at her again, calculating, measuring. "As quick as my former relationships, you mean."

"I have noticed the tendency," she murmured, slowly withdrawing her hand. She bent a dried piece of grass between her fingers till it snapped. She picked out the shorter stalk.

"You believe I'm some kind of Romeo?"

"Can a hundred newspapers be wrong?"

"If newspapers were right, we'd be in bed by now."

She frowned. "Okay, so maybe all the stories weren't true, but you haven't exactly been a monk for ten years."

"No." He grinned. They'd been dalliances, nothing more, nothing like this.

Mariah tried to quell the way her heart turned over at his smile.

"But I won't fill you in on the gruesome details," he added with a short bow.

"Thanks loads."

He laughed. She laughed. Why was it so hard to

stay angry with him, to resist when she knew it was the only way?

"What's wrong, really, Stash? Be honest with me, that's all I ask."

"In dancing, as in life, you're a woman who demands the most difficult things."

"It's just that underneath that public persona you can be very secretive."

"That goes without saying."

"Secrets usually do."

"Where I come from, you don't let everyone see the deepest part of you. Is safer that way."

"So I would have to accept that if we were . . . involved."

"It's unfair, I know. Especially when I want you because you're so very open."

She felt just that way when he touched her; a flower at sunrise, petals unfolding and dotted with dew. "I hoped the rumors about us would evaporate of their own accord once we were out of New York."

"You say I move too fast. Going halfway is not my nature. I want you, that is all." It was everything.

Mariah let out a long breath. "We have to work together."

"Dance together."

She shivered, then stood up, wrapping her towel around her waist and knotting it. "It is possible for a man and woman to work together without sex taking over."

"Then what is the point?"

"Is that why you joined the company?"

Yes. No. How could he answer? "Why do you fight me on this? Making love is one of the things that gives life a meaning. Like dancing—if you can, you do. You find the right partner and rejoice. We should leave all this talk behind and just do it." An autocratic motion with his hand cut off all discussion. Then he smiled. He was proud of that. It was a decision, a choice. It was practically a speech, and he'd said it very well.

Mariah felt her mouth freeze at the corners. What a line! Not only did he deliver it perfectly, now he had the gall to stand there as if he expected applause.

"I'm supposed to shut up and make love with you, right?"

His pleased smile faded. "Not those words exactly."

"*That* is despicable."

His brows shot up as if he were truly surprised. "Then it is not what I meant."

"No?" She kicked into her sandals. Sand spurted up behind her heels as she strode toward her cabin.

"Darling, wait!"

Darlink. "Oh, Bullwinkle!"

The low, mournful notes of a cello emanated from between the trees. At least one other person was up, she thought, and sounded about as miserable as she felt.

At last Stash had come right out and named his terms: a dance partner was expected to be a bed partner. He really did want to dance naked! Well, she wasn't so accommodating. She'd made that clear from the start.

He came up behind her, his steps hushed on the sandy path. Cabin screens were open on all sides of them, curtains fluttering softly in a warm breeze. Mariah was wet and chilled. She needed a shower to get rid of the sand. She didn't need a roll in the hay.

"I said it wrong." His voice was low, raspy.

"I don't want to hear it. We have a contract, we dance together, that's all."

"Let me say it differently."

"Stash, every time you open your mouth you put one of your insured feet into it. I suggest you—"

Her suggestion was cut off by his hand on her shoulder, swinging her around. His lips met hers as she stumbled against his chest. He pulled back only long enough to murmur, "I say it better like this."

His mouth returned to hers, hard, hot, and deep. There was nothing subtle this time. No investigation of compatibility. It was a raw example of a strictly masculine need to take.

And to Mariah's regret, it quickly met a woman's need to give.

His tongue was in her mouth. Every part of her that was liquid or could become so heated and flowed, contrasting with the cold, congealing damp of her bathing suit. The cloth brushed against his skin with a sibilant whisper. His towel, slung around his shoulders, pressed her breasts. In seconds the heat of him came through. His hardness pressed against the knot at her waist.

She felt all of it, and it all dissolved when she touched him, one hand splayed on his shoulder blades, the other on his neck, her fingertips lost in the midnight of his hair.

Tactile and immediate, there was no halfway about touching him. But none of it could distract her from the way his mouth possessed hers, plundering her resolve. A languid droplet of water slipped between her thighs. With a quiet gasp she felt him catch it on his thumb and spread it higher.

She quivered in his arms. His strength she had; she wanted the emotion. "Give me," she said, only half realizing she'd spoken. *Tell me how you feel.* "Show me."

One move from him and her towel fell to the ground.

An alarm clock shattered the morning quiet. Mariah jumped. No wonder they armed time bombs that way; she felt as if one had just gone off somewhere in the vicinity of her solar plexus.

Someone turned the damned thing off.

The shattered silence had nothing on Stash's look. "Let me dance with you. Move with me, Mariah. I didn't come this far to take no for an answer."

He turned without a good-bye and walked in the direction of his cabin. Mariah swallowed the taste of him in her mouth, the feel of him still shivering on her nearly bare skin.

It must have been seven A.M. Alarms seemed to be sounding all over the camp. Very real, very close, very loud alarms.

Six

He must have planned it. It was the only explanation Mariah could come up with. Never mind he hadn't known she'd swim that day. Never mind his need had been palpably real . . .

As real as hers, a voice whispered.

And apparently as spontaneous. As combustible.

He had to know, she argued, crossing the bustling camp to the dance building. He'd been doing a lot of work with Danny. Today was the first time in two weeks she'd scheduled the time to work directly with him. Tonight they'd be dancing onstage—not together, but close enough.

Of all the days to find him alone at the lake. Of all the days to kiss him until the top of her head was ready to come off. Of all the days to wrap herself around him like—

She halted in the doorway of the pine-paneled room. The wall of mirrors reflected two dancers, the music reflected love and yearning. The lithe young woman had one leg wrapped around Danny's torso, the other pointed in a line parallel to his. He held her in one arm, lowering her, lowering her. Her hair swept the floor, her face upside down.

"Mariah! About time." Shelly squirmed around.

Danny grabbed her. "Hold on or I'll drop you."

"No, you won't. You're a golden-glove fielder, right? Never dropped a dancer in your life."

"There's always a first."

He swung her upright and set her on her toe shoes.

"We decided to get in some studio time," she said to Mariah.

"All of ten minutes," Danny added.

The morning class had cleared out fifteen minutes earlier. It was a tight schedule, but Mariah had managed to clear a two-hour block for the lunch period.

She set down her dance bag. "Stash here?"

Why ask? she wondered. He obviously wasn't. Star presence like his had a way of making the air hum, among other things, like pulses, heartbeats.

"He'll be here," Danny said. "He went into town."

"Town?"

Danny shrugged. "I'm his roommate, not his keeper. He went looking for a *New York Times*."

Shelly laughed and draped her arm through Danny's, giggling in his ear with all the urgency of a seventeen-year-old on a diplomatic mission of great delicacy. Something, Mariah knew, about her waking up to find her own roommate gone at an ungodly hour of the morning.

Lacing a shoe, Mariah caught Danny's curious look in the mirror. "All right, you two," she said, tugging up a pink leg warmer. "Enough conspiracy. We're going to work on the new duet. It was supposed to be Shelly and Stash."

"But you want me to learn it in case," Danny said.

"In case. Some nights you'll go on instead of Stash."

"And some nights you instead of me," Shelly put in. "Better make it good and sexy."

Mariah smiled tightly, riffling through the tapes beside the tape deck. She might dance this one with Danny. She had no intention of doing it with Stash.

Doing it with Stash. The implications of the phrase made her grimace. She sounded like Shelly. Clapping her hands, she snapped them all back to attention. "Let's get started."

No one moved. Stash was standing in the doorway.

"Glad you could join us," Mariah said, her voice ringing hollowly in the big room.

He said little, smiled less. It was obvious he'd come to work. He dropped his ratty dance bag on the low platform by the piano, a folded newspaper poking out of the broken zipper. Donning his dance slippers, he took his place on the floor. "Who is my partner?"

"You'll be solo for the exhibition tonight. I'd like you to dance *Cocteau Cocktail*. Do you feel up to it?"

"Sure."

"Shelly, you and Danny will do *Rondelay* and *Stitch in Time*."

"Gotcha," Danny replied.

"Then I'll do *Since I Fell*. It'll be a short program,

but that should show off what we've got to work with.

"So, we'll run through those, then I want to use most of our time today blocking out the new stuff. Stash, could you dance with Shelly?" She knew by his look he'd rather dance with her. That had been her own plan, until that morning's kiss.

He gave a "very well" shrug, then smiled at the teenager beside him and nodded toward the mirrors. "We look good together."

Shelly tipped up her chin, pretending to study them. But, like a nervous filly, her eyes kept shying to the man beside her. With an air of ultrasophistication, she exhaled and tried again. "We do."

"We shall."

Charm, Mariah thought, watching. He didn't pour it on, he smoothed it on, like suntan lotion. And Shelly beamed and bloomed under it. Fluttering between adoration and feigned indifference, she partnered him for the next hour while Mariah used Danny to block out the new moves.

It was grinding work, mostly repetition. They counted beats, memorized motions pieced together step by step. There was little emotion at this point. The song played over in the background.

"Turn on six, seven, eight, lift your knee then your foot, no, don't point yet, extend your arm at the same time. No, sorry, do it again, let me see."

Shelly, the classical ballerina Mariah would never be, looked wonderful beside Stash. Mariah worked them harder. So what if he was smiling at the girl? He'd promised not to trifle with her emotions. But how could he help it? She was giggling and laughing and plainly showing off, and Mariah doubted it was for her sake.

"Shelly, mind paying attention here? You're too fluttery and you're counting it wrong."

Wrong choice of words. Despite the air of mature indifference, Shelly was thin-skinned and easily bruised. First she got pouty, then stiff, then angry.

"Try it again."

"That was my fault, Mariah."

"I'm not placing blame, Stash, I just want to see it again. Correctly if possible."

"Dance it yourself!" Shelly ran to the barre, tears of frustration breaking free, sobbing all the harder because she couldn't control them.

Mariah talked to her quietly. "Comes with the territory, Shel. I'm not going to baby you."

"You don't have to embarrass me."

"I can't send Stash out of the room every time I correct you."

"It isn't—" She backed down, sullenly staring at Danny lighting a cigarette.

"Besides," Mariah added, "you're dancing for him, not me."

"What does that mean?"

"In rehearsals, I'm the audience, it's me you have to impress. You're dancing like you have one eye on Stash all the time."

"He's my partner. And who's impressing who anyway? He's your big star, you've got to keep him happy."

"I thought we were having this argument because I was picking on *you* too much."

"Forget it. I'd rather dance with Danny."

Oh, brother. "Why don't you sit this one out?"

Shelly seized her dance bag instead, marching out with head held high.

Mariah called after her. "Remember the group class at three. I'd like you here so the students can see how a professional behaves."

Danny and Stash were sitting on the floor, backs to the mirror. Steam from their bodies outlined them in the glass. Four new numbers to work out over eight weeks, and two weeks already gone. Sighing, Mariah took a seat beside them on the floor. "I played that wrong."

"Maybe I should go after her," Danny said.

Not sure she wanted to be left alone with Stash, Mariah sighed again. "Would you mind?"

Danny was up and out.

"It was partly my fault," Stash said. He'd been watching Mariah, the way she stood, the way she danced, the tilt of her head when she was thinking. "My concentration isn't good today," he explained. "I was messing her up."

"It might be easier if you didn't flirt with her so much."

"We're dancing."

"And that's all part of it, huh? As casual as that. Well, it isn't to her."

"Or to you?"

"Let's stay on the subject, shall we? I asked you not to interfere with her."

He muttered an oath in Russian. "I will dance with my fingertips and toes. You won't even know I'm there."

"I'm serious. She's a delicate girl."

"And you're not?"

Mariah scowled as if the answer were perfectly obvious. She was a woman and could take care of herself. She had other people to look out for, feelings to protect. "Never mind," she said. "I don't want to get into this right now."

Neither did Stash. He felt guilty enough as it was. When he danced with Shelly he thought only of Mariah in his arms, Mariah touching him that way, Mariah watching. He hadn't thought for a moment the girl had taken him seriously. He still wasn't sure she had.

The silence stretched. They waited for Danny to return with Shelly. It didn't look as though it was going to happen anytime soon.

Mariah studied the row of windows above the barre, knowing the lake was only twenty or thirty feet away. A splash sounded off the floating dock, followed by shouts and laughter. Her concentration had blocked the sounds out until then, like the orchestra rehearsing next door, or the way the afternoon humidity sat on her skin. "Stuffy in here."

"Mmm."

She needed a diversion from his silence, a way to break the discomfort. Plucking at the folds of his thick sweat pants, careful not to actually touch the leg underneath, she said, "I hope you don't plan on marketing *these* in your line of dancewear."

"Sportswear. If it's called dancewear, men won't buy it."

"Ah. The subtleties of language."

"I learn a little every day." But not enough to tell her how he felt.

"So it's all marketing."

"Selling is everything," he intoned gravely. "Am I breaking her heart?"

Mariah shook her head. "Shelly doesn't know what her heart wants yet."

"Except to dance."

"Right now it wants to take a couple hours off before I paddle her behind."

"And what does your heart want?"

Mariah ignored the possibilities. "I came here to get some work done."

"Here we are." He shrugged. His arm brushed hers with the motion.

She hadn't realized they were so close. She sat up straighter. Her back, bare in the lowcut leotard, squeaked against the mirror.

His gaze held her. "Work with me," he said.

It sounded like *live with me, love with me, be with me.* She read all of that in his eyes, remembering the alarms.

"All right," She hauled herself up, leaving her sweater in a pile behind her, and marched to the center of the room. "Let's try, 'You Don't Send Me Flowers.'"

He flipped through the tapes while she limbered up.

"We'll take it slow," she said, watching him in the mirrored wall as he walked up behind her.

She thought she glimpsed a knowing smile at her words. When she turned, he was serious. He placed his hands professionally on her waist, moving her left, right, toward him. On her toes, she leaned in, almost brushing her breasts against his chest. Almost. He set her back on her feet. He looked into her eyes for two beats.

Her heart pounded as if they'd been working for hours.

She had to drag her gaze away from his, watch

the mirror, work on the patterns. Concentrate on how to express the emotions of two people who'd lost track of how to communicate with each other.

You don't send me flowers.

He turned her face to his with his palm. She looked up at him in blank surprise. His mouth was inches away.

He took it no further.

"Again," she said, her throat tight and dry.

They took it from the top.

Never, never did he hold her any closer than he had to. Even when she clung to him, sliding down his body, he merely drew her up, assumed the next position, held her exactly as she asked to be held and no more.

There was a subterranean beat in the music to which her pulse was adding bongo drums. Tension mounted, and never stepped across the line.

Stash," she said, breathing hard, leaning against him, watching the beat of a pulse against his neck, the beading of sweat on his brow.

They danced but didn't touch, seducing each other artfully, artificially.

"What do you want?" he murmured, every movement precise, exact, and cold. But his body wasn't. The desire building inside him was as palpable as the outline of his body in the thin black tights he'd stripped down to. "Tell me what to do," he whispered.

"Kiss me before I go crazy."

It was what he wanted to hear. Carefully, fully intending to do only what she asked and no more, he complied.

It was true, she wanted him to kiss her. And because it was true, it was strong, honest. It cut through all the pretenses she'd built up to keep him at bay. It was as needy and vulnerable as the request that had brought it on. And she didn't care.

One arm went around his neck, the other under his arm, her hand splayed against his shoulder blade. He bent her back, dipping, making her heart plunge and bubbles and stars burst in her veins, as if he were laying her back in a bed, and she was ready to be under him.

She moaned his name.

His chest was sweaty and fragrant with the smell of man. His tongue parted her lips, found and parried with hers. Mouths promising bodies with an emotion so primal, she had no way of containing it. Teeth bit and teased, sharp and edgy.

He had to pull back for air. His lungs burned as if he'd been holding his breath. The rest of him blazed too. His skin was raspy as sandpaper, itching to be soothed by hers, hers that was so cool, belying the flames in her cheeks, the sparkle in her eyes.

He'd been chasing her so long, and now she was his. "You do want me." There was no way he could hold back, not crow in triumph.

Her hair was slick under his palm, secured in a chignon he wanted to undo but didn't. After all, it bared her cheeks, her ear, the white slope of her neck. He would bare the rest, her collarbone, her shoulder dotted with faint freckles. He was amazed at the way his hand quaked on the edge of her leotard. He pushed it down, his fingertips brushing the indentation the elasticized edge had left on her skin.

She was touching him like a woman, surrendering like one.

He stripped off the leotard until it stretched to her elbow, holding her arm to her side. A lacy pink cup was revealed, a breast coaxed free for his hand, his mouth.

She groaned his name and threw her head back, clutching at him.

The music clicked off at the end of the tape. In the big room it echoed as sharp and hard as a slamming door.

Mariah looked up and saw Shelly running past the main window. She held Stash's head, but he'd seen too.

"Shelly."

"Now I've done it," he said.

"No, it wasn't your fault."

"Want me to talk to her?"

"I'll see her tonight."

"And me?" He grabbed her arm. "Mariah, you're not stopping now."

"I can't believe we came all the way out here so I could deny the rumors in the papers, only to make them come true."

"What if they are? What if we're meant to be?"

"I'm not sure I believe in that kind of fate. If I did, I'd believe I was never cut out to be a dancer."

"But you kept trying. *We* have to. There has to be a common language."

"Is that our problem?" She stuffed the tapes into her dance bag.

He touched her breast, now covered again. She froze, his hand cupping her.

"When I tell you this"—he pressed softly—"you

know what I mean. These are our words. Can you deny it?"

Not anywhere near as much as she wanted to. "Stash."

"We have what we have, now, no past getting in the way." And no future? He wouldn't think about it. "We need to be lovers."

"Why?"

"Because otherwise we cannot dance together. Dance with me tonight."

"We haven't rehearsed anything together."

"What we just did."

"You want *that* onstage? It's barely complete and what's there was mostly improvising."

"It's true. It's emotion. That's what you want."

That wasn't what she wanted from him. What she wanted was deeper and more frightening, and she knew she had no right to expect it. "I don't think I'm ready to go public with that number."

"Or us."

"Yes."

"And after tonight's performance?"

She looked into his eyes. "What about it? You dance your number, I'll dance mine. And Shelly, if she hasn't run away, will dance hers with Danny."

He shook his head briskly. "I mean, will you go straight to bed afterward?"

"Is that an invitation?"

He watched the battle in her eyes. She was hoping he'd come out with it and say yes. And she'd have an excuse to say no. The language between men and women was even more complicated than English.

"I will wait until after the performance for your answer," he said.

Mariah walked out of the rehearsal hall. She had until that night to decide if she and Stash were going to be lovers. But first she'd have to watch him dance. She stopped at a fountain and took a long drink of cold mineral-tasting water. Unable to hide anything she felt while dancing, she'd had the misfortune of getting involved with a man who was a master at dance, at provoking, arousing.

She could always say no, she thought grimly.

But her body would be saying yes.

The performance went fine. Shelly showed up surly and subdued, but she danced with headlong bravado. In one quick exit, Danny winked at Mariah backstage, took a series of deep breaths, then ran back out, his words trailing after him.

"You really lit a fire under Shelly today."

Mariah grimaced. Now, if only she could put it out. The performance seemed to be flying by and there was no way to postpone it. Stash wanted an answer. Although she pretended to be too busy to talk, his smoldering looks wouldn't let the issue die. Even when he danced the comic *Cocteau Cocktail*, he imbued it with enough sensuality and self-assured flair to leave every woman in the audience chuckling and fantasizing at the same time.

Mariah strode out to take her place as soon as the curtain swung shut. Stash passed her on the way and grasped her arm, the remainder of his ovation still scattered throughout the auditorium. He kissed her full on the lips, then let her go.

Standing in the blackness, waiting for her spotlight, she seriously wondered if her legs would ever move again. Then the music started.

Since I Fell for You. The question of her life played to a packed hall. Had she fallen for Stash? Yes. *When* was the real question. It could have been anywhere between here and New York, between the ages of fifteen and twenty-eight. It could have been his laughter and teasing, his assurance, his simmering sexuality. The easy answer was his dancing. The harder one was his touch. The one she barely acknowledged was her own need. He appealed to her, astonished her, excited her. And he wouldn't let go.

Every time she put him on a pedestal and said don't touch, he touched. Every time she convinced herself she wasn't his type, he stepped down and took her in his arms. The song ought to end with a surrender, not a joke.

Up to that point he'd called all the shots, and darn her if she hadn't answered.

So she took control, she improvised. Walking into the darkness outside her shrinking spotlight as the saxophone wound down, she stretched out her hand, open to the next possibility, and the next, willing to risk despite all misgivings.

The applause shook her out of her frozen stance. She went back on for three quick bows. But only one pair of hands mattered—Stash's.

"You've found the ending," he murmured, his arm around her.

It might just be the beginning, she thought.

Seven

Amore was a signature piece Stash had brought with him. Daring, breathtaking, flagrant. It was blatant and bold seduction, erotic and powerful and public. He was a man about to claim a woman and he didn't care who knew it. He finished with a leap that had Mariah's heart in her throat. The crowd roared.

Stash bowed, sweat-dampened locks of hair falling over his face. He swept them back with a flourish. Oh, he was good at this, she thought. She could almost hear the women sigh. Or had that been her?

Danny tapped her on the shoulder. The entire company had to take bows. Stash escorted her to the edge of the stage and lifted up a bouquet of roses to present to her.

When the curtain finally hushed shut, all the air went out of her lungs.

"The performance was great, wasn't it?" Shelly asked.

"Damn great." Danny clapped Stash on the back, then Mariah. "Too bad we can't go someplace for a drink to celebrate."

"I believe Mariah and I will be celebrating alone," Stash said.

Mariah felt the flush in her cheeks. "We have some things to discuss, Dan."

"Great. Well, Shelly and I are headed into town anyway, see what's still open."

"Have fun."

"Same to you." The lanky Texan grinned as he steered Shelly toward the dressing rooms.

Stash looked at Mariah. He made all the proper remarks to the people milling around them, but his gaze seldom left her for long. "Are we ready?" he finally asked.

"We have to mingle awhile longer."

"I'm game. Are you?"

It was obvious he was talking about more than after-performance chitchat. "Stash—"

"We'll talk." He was the impresario again, taking her by the shoulders and leading her through the crowd, showing her off, taking charge.

For the moment she was too exhausted to fight. She'd figured it out onstage, the need to have a say in whatever was to become of this relationship, the need not to let him call all the shots. And the need, equally real, equally pressing, to take the risk, to improvise when emotion demanded it.

Stash opened the small refrigerator in the corner of the cabin and pulled out a diet soda and a beer, the latter for him, the former for Mariah. It was past midnight, but the flush of performance had yet to wear off. He still felt the high that came with dancing, a combination of physical effort and emotional reward. It tingled deep in the muscles, skittered along the skin. Relief and exhilaration mixed with exhaustion and leftover adrenaline. Sparks waited to give off heat while she sat in his cabin.

Mariah had to be feeling it too.

She looked up as if he'd spoken aloud. When he didn't, she cleared her throat. "I need to have some say in what's happening to us."

"Please do."

"Stash, you walk into my life, act as if we're destined to be lovers, and expect me just to lie down for it."

He raised a brow.

"Let me reword that."

"No, no. I like."

"You have the wrong idea about me, although heaven knows I've tried to make myself clear."

"I've said it the best I know how. If I'm not getting through . . ."

Oh, yes, he was. And it was scaring her to death.

Stash sensed she was delicate and knew she'd deny it. She hid it somewhere inside that big sweater, inside the tight-fitting faded jeans. Her hair was free and loose, brushed to a soft red gleam that whispered across her shoulders. She looked as flushed as if she'd just had sex. As nervous as if they were about to.

"Nice place," she said, making a face.

He laughed and actually took the time to glance around at the pine paneling, the dotted Swiss curtains, the chenille bedspread any mother would be comfortable with. Mariah looked as if she expected satin sheets and a bear rug, with teeth.

He set down his beer. "We could share."

Her gaze ricocheted from the bed to the table. "Oh, I'll stick with soda. Thanks."

"Anytime."

"As for our talking." She became engrossed in the enamel surface of the small table. "You know why I'm here."

"I have hopes." He grinned and turned a chair around, straddling it. The smile didn't stay on his face long. She looked beat, hopeless, as if she'd given up a fight. He didn't want her coming to him that way.

"I think it's time we settled what's been happening between us," she said.

"Ever since you came into the company, you've acted as if we'd be lovers. You seem to have some picture of me."

"It's a very beautiful picture. A woman who dances naked, who shares her emotions."

"What I share onstage is what I practice. I'm controlling it. I'm not like that in real life. You've worked with me, seen me offstage." Mariah couldn't believe her ears. It was as if she were the star and he the lovestruck fan who had to be set right. "I'm not what you want, Stash."

"You think by now I don't know what I want when I see it?"

"I think you've seen a heckuva lot more than I have. For someone five years older than me, you've been so many places, done so much . . ."

"With so many women." He smiled.

She didn't. "These other women were all classical dancers, or stars—"

"You'll be joining them soon."

Them or him? "I meant, they're all so elegant, experienced. I've let the company take up most of my time. I haven't really devoted that much to polishing my social skills. You'd be bored with me in a matter of weeks." There, she thought, that ought to do it. Honesty might be the best policy, but it was also sheer hell. "I want you to believe me."

He nodded. It was clear she was sincere about this. And thoroughly wrong. Once she'd been told she'd never be a classical dancer, that she didn't measure up, and despite the applause, the growing success, part of her still believed it.

He sipped his beer, wishing it were vodka. He didn't want to be her judge; he wanted to be her lover.

She drained half her soda in one long gulp and demurely camouflaged a hiccup. "I guess what I'm trying to say is that you seem to want more than I have to give. I'm not . . . experienced that way."

He smiled, carefully hiding how shaken he felt. She'd told him she'd once been ashamed of being a woman, but that couldn't mean she'd never enjoyed, never tried . . .

"Believe me," she went on, "it doesn't do much to a woman's ego to admit this, but there it is."

"You're being honest with me, Mariah. For that I thank you very much." He touched her hand. "You are a virgin. I respect this, although it surprises me. I would be honored to teach you. And very deeply moved."

"Very deeply" was how he was trying to look into her eyes when her mouth dropped open and she laughed.

He blinked, disconcerted, then proceeded cautiously. "If I've been rushing you, I promise I can take it slow, Mariah."

"Stash, I am *not* a virgin!" Hearing people pass by outside, she immediately lowered her voice. "I've had, I mean I've . . . well, nothing lasting, but that doesn't mean . . . I wouldn't measure up." And never had. That embarrassed, mortified girl whose own body had betrayed her still existed. And having the most handsome man she'd ever known look at her with desire in his eyes only made her more aware of her inadequacies.

"I can practice what I do onstage," she said, "but how can I practice around you? You know these steps backward and forward. I'm not your speed. You'd leave me in the dust."

"I wouldn't leave you," he said quietly. Wouldn't he? Part of him was less than sure. Part of him didn't want to make promises he couldn't keep, not to this woman. "You think I want only to sweep you off your feet?"

She didn't answer.

"All right," he said, addressing her and his conscience. "I'll tell you truth as I know it. I think I may be falling in love with you."

Her reaction was far from what he'd hoped. He expected surprise, anger, passion if he was lucky. Instead, he got measured words.

"You fall in love with all the women you dance with," she began carefully. "You're very loyal to them too. I don't hold that against you. That's one of your good qualities."

"You sound unhappy I have them."

"Believe me, this would be a lot easier if you didn't."

"Wouldn't it be easier to love?"

"It seldom is."

"It would be more fun to dance that way."

Until he could no longer dance. She had known that coming in; he was there until his knee gave out. Dance was everything to him. When the career was over, he'd find another life. It wouldn't include her.

Did that mean she'd watch him go, having kept the boundaries firmly drawn, having denied herself his touch? His friendship? And now his love? The sense of loss was keen, the premature regret even worse.

His voice was raspy, low. "You said once, you don't know what you want in a dance until you see it danced."

"Meaning?"

"You won't know if you love me until we make love."

She laughed, although she didn't feel like it. "I think I'd know, Stash."

"Is like an arranged marriage, yes? We meet and marry when I join your company, we sign the contract. Then we get to know each other and love comes."

Too true, she thought. But it came mixed up with desire and need and flat-out adoration, watching him move, laugh, tease the other dancers, work with the kids. Who'd have guessed he had the patience to teach? The young dancers at the camp followed him around as if he were a movie star, staying late in the sessions he'd generously agreed to take on, learning everything they could while he was there because he'd soon be gone.

Mariah knew the feeling. She suddenly wanted everything he could give, precisely because he would go.

He got up, empty bottle in his hand. She reached out to touch his fingers. "Stash?"

One word, one name. One man she'd loved in so many ways for so long. Never this way, or this much, or so physically she ached with it.

It was a long reach; she hadn't quite touched him. He had to step forward for her fingertips to brush the back of his hand. Something quivered inside him, something warm. He frowned and held her hand, then let it drop.

He closed the windows and pulled the curtains. In the clutter of tapes he found a jazzy, slow one. Suddenly impatient with the setting, he tugged off the bedspread, turned the lamp to low, then off, then low again. The less time they might have, the more perfect he wanted it to be. He paced to the foot of the bed to pick up the spread—it didn't look good like that, he didn't want it like that—but he gave up halfway there.

She remained at the table, watching as the low boots he wore ticked against the old linoleum. His legs were lean inside black designer jeans. His turtleneck was black, his hair darker than the night outside. There was fury in him, leashed energy, and she didn't give a damn about how the cabin looked.

She stood up, her wavering courage making her legs as unsteady as a newborn colt's, and walked over to him. She put her hands on his waist, then up under the light sweater until she found skin. "I never knew you were so fussy." It was meant to be teasing, but her voice was husky.

"I want it to be right."

So did she. Her entire being told her it was. "Then kiss me like you did this afternoon."

He refused, and a smile curved one side of his mouth at her surprise. "Dance with me first."

It started chaste. Gently swaying, his hands on her hips, her arms loose around his neck. An entire song played low and bluesy while they learned each other a step at a time.

He moved in closer, meeting the glancing touch of her body. He lifted her sweater over her head. "We'll dance naked. You in my arms. Me inside you. Do you want that, Mariah?"

She murmured something against his neck. The turtleneck would have to go; it covered too much of him. But right now she delighted in the feel of it, the light layer of fuzz, warmed from the inside, teasing her, delicate, unlike the searing sensation of his touch when he flattened his hands against her back.

"You rub against me like a cat," he murmured.

"I love this sweater."

"Love me."

No arguments. The sweater was off.

"And these?" She teased, her hands floating down to the waistband of his black jeans. "They look awfully good to me, Stash. Very tight."

"And getting tighter."

She smiled a lazy smile. All her insecurities and doubts could be pushed aside as long as he looked at her with his flashing dark eyes.

She danced away from him; he tugged her in closer, using the tab on her zipper. It slid down. They said good-bye to the jeans, his hands sliding over the firm muscles of her buttocks, lowering, clenching, his jaw set and tight when he saw the flimsy lace that remained.

The music wasn't loud enough. He wanted harder, faster, something propulsive to match the way his body felt.

She undid his belt. While her fingers slid down his zipper without undoing it, her mouth made a trail all its own across his bared chest.

It was as if a depth charge had gone off deep inside him. The music was obliterated by the sound of his labored breathing, even by the sight of her faint smile. She licked her lips as if perfectly satisfied.

He wasn't. He grasped her arms and held her away from him. The cabin was stuffy and hot. Perspiration from the evening's performance had been stemmed by a quick shower, but it was back, simmering just below his skin, sheening on hers. Her nipples were smooth, rosy, and wet. He'd been kissing them, could still taste them in his mouth. He kissed them again, and felt the way her abdomen moved as she took little startled breaths.

"The bed," he said, his voice hoarse with effort.

She nodded.

They stripped off the rest of their clothes and found the sheets cool in comparison to each other's skin. He reached across her, tilting the tape deck precariously as he turned the tape over. The drawer of the nightstand squeaked in the sticky heat as he pulled out the only protection they'd need. Everything else was bare, everything else was vulnerable.

It was a new dance, and very old, made up of horizontal lines and lingering touches, of tightened muscles held rigid before they could yield. Advance and retreat. Surrender and triumph.

Each touch singed her like a brushfire through grass, bending and surging before the wind. Like music, rising and falling, climbing slowly to the crescendo.

They entwined and parted, finding new ways. When he reared back, she watched him in the dim light. He was slick and shining, every line taut. Her hand joined his, smoothing the latex on, and she thought of the way emotion was revealed in movement, the things only bodies could say.

His hair was damp and clinging, his eyes bottomless. Her mystery wasn't nearly so deep. It was open to him and vulnerable, especially now, with the gentleness rapidly waning.

He wanted. He'd have.

She wanted. And so she'd give.

"Mariah."

Something turned over inside her, melting, flowing like lava. When he joined her, his breath hot and harsh, his body hard and spearing, he met a partner who could dance this dance, match his rhythm.

Or counter it, with the lazy, maddening circles her hips made, her legs gripping his waist, the unutterably thrilling feel of her moving beneath him, with him. Her shuddering delight reverberated through him, followed by the shock of her tears, glistening on her faint brown lashes, her whispered "please, please." He knew in one thundering flash that she was there and he could no longer hold back. He raced to meet her, a stroke, two, his blood pounding. She looked at him in love, and the stars themselves couldn't have produced the light that filled him, the explosion that rocked him.

He shuddered again in her arms, the sweat at his temples mingling with her tears.

Alarm swept through him. He couldn't have hurt her. "Darling."

She sighed and smiled. She could get used to *darlink*. It was downright endearing. Unlike the man who slowly withdrew and lay beside her in the narrow bed. He'd been passionate, unrelenting, unapologetic. Nothing he'd shown her could be classified with a word as lighthearted as endearing. And yet . . .

He lifted his head to kiss the corner of her eyelid. "You are all right?" Not quite a question.

She weakly lifted a hand and ran it down the center of his chest. Not quite an answer, but it would have to do.

Catching her hand, he held it against his navel. She felt the rise and fall of him, his breathing slowed almost to normal.

"What are you thinking?" he asked.

"That you recover fast. I'm still quaking."

He smiled, a male-too-pleased-with-himself smile. "I do."

"Do what?"

"Recover fast." He rolled on his side, head held jauntily on his palm, and leered for all he was worth.

Mariah laughed until the bed shook. "Well, I guess I can't match you there, so don't even think it!"

"We've got to practice if we're going to get this

right. Isn't that what the Lady Mariah tells me so often?"

"That's in rehearsal."

"And what is this?"

"This, buster, was more like opening night." Complete with jitters, second thoughts, and sheer terror. She grinned and touched his face, feeling the hint of stubble. "Maybe that's why I get the feeling I should stand up and applaud."

He quickly draped a forearm across her waist. "May I offer my own *brava*?"

"Thank you," she said softly.

"I'd give you your roses all over again."

He *did* send her flowers. "They were from you, then."

"They will be every night, every time we dance. I must please my partner." He nipped at her shoulder.

"And if your partner has thorns?"

"I'll still love her petals"—he touched her intimately—"and the way they bloom. Like a rose covered with dew when night falls."

She shuddered and stopped his hand. Although her lips parted, no sound came out save for a shuddering breath.

"I love you," he whispered, cheating, saying it in Russian, not expecting her to understand.

From somewhere she found the only word that mattered as she reached for him. "Stash."

"If I fall asleep, promise you'll wake me," she'd said, a smile playing over her lips, her lids already heavy.

"I will," he'd promised. Even as he'd said it, though, he'd had no intention of doing so.

But she believed him. She trusted him. When Mariah gave it was freely, no strings, no conditions. The respect with which she held her emotions, the care, were expected to be returned.

Stash frowned, torn between wanting to touch her, yet not disturb her. He'd turned off the light, and the moon trailed its long silver rays over them. He envied the way they lit on her skin, softly illuminating.

How many women had he known? None like this. That she wasn't so easily won shouldn't have surprised him. What shook him were the emotions she aroused in him every time he thought of her, even when lying in bed, letting the pain in his knee distract him until he had to get up. How would he ever sleep again without her?

She wanted to be more than a woman he danced with. She was. In rehearsals she'd demanded emotions from him and got them. Now he'd shown her she could reveal those same emotions in bed, with him. A fair trade? If he expected it to buy him some credit with his conscience, it didn't. Because he wasn't giving her the same honesty.

Yes, he was loyal to his partners, faithful to his friends. He was also a defector, selfish and disloyal. He'd betrayed his country and deserted his family. Headlines from home branded him a traitor in his native language. If he truly loved Mariah, wouldn't he protect her from such a man?

"The people I love most are the ones I leave behind. Know that, Mariah," he whispered in the dark. "Protect some part of yourself."

She stirred.

He grew quiet.

She'd be angry when she woke and found he'd let her sleep in his bed all night.

She would see he couldn't always be taken at his word. What better way to learn the lesson defectors taught?

Eight

It had to be very late, one, maybe two A.M., and so quiet she could hear the lake. Even the breeze seemed to have drifted off to sleep. Mariah listened to Stash breathing beside her and knew he was awake—another curious form of intimacy, that knowing, that awareness. She opened her eyes to the moonlight.

"Sorry," she whispered. "I drifted off."

"I don't mind."

"I should be going. Danny will be back."

"And Shelly."

Mariah frowned. When you lived and breathed your work, it was never far away. "What are we going to do about her? She has a terrible crush on you."

"I don't know about that."

"Surely you have a lot of experience with girls having crushes on you?"

"She likes me, of course."

"Of course." No ego there, she thought, smiling indulgently.

"But as for love . . ." He shrugged, idly skimming his fingers over her bare skin. "Will you dance with me again?"

Her mouth formed a little O.

"I mean over there." He indicated the open section of floor with a toss of his head.

She reached automatically to push back the lock of black hair that tumbled on his forehead, luxuriating in the intimacy that gave her the right.

"We'll dance the number you wanted me to do with Shelly," he said.

"I can't take it away from her. Unless it would take some of the pressure off her for the premiere. It might also teach her a lesson in professionalism." She sighed. "Not an easy choice."

"If you teach me here, I can dance it better. Then I can help her and you won't yell at her so much."

Mariah groaned. "I don't yell."

"You think we can't tell when you're unhappy? You show disapproval with the little line between your eyes, like this." Standing stark naked, Stash did a dead-on imitation of her in front of her rehearsing dancers, tapping her foot, arms crossed, frowning.

"I do *not* look like that!" Mariah howled and flopped back on the bed, a pillow thrown over her face.

"You do. Come. We dance it again until I have it in this thick skull of mine."

She couldn't refuse. He was standing, feet turned out and legs together, arm extended palm-up, as if waiting for the music to begin for *Les Sylphides* or any other great ballet. The only difference was that this dancer had forgotten his tights.

"Let me slip these on," she said, reaching for her lace panties.

"No."

"Ah, he's ordering me around already."

"Dance to please me, that is all I ask." Spoken in a stark commanding tone worthy of the king of Siam.

Mariah set her mouth in a thin line and walked over to the tape deck. She carefully kept the volume low. Beneath her bare feet, the braided rug was warm and gritty with sand as she crossed back to Stash. Dancing naked was one thing when it was part of a seduction, but this—"You expect me to be as unselfconscious about my body as you are."

"No reason not to be."

"Mine isn't as perfect as yours."

"It is. In every way." His fingertips ticked off a few examples. "You need more lessons? I'll show you." His arms went around her, and his kiss was deep and possessive, brooking no argument, even if she'd been left with the words to make one. "You are complete, sexy, beautiful." He was handling her breasts, lifting, sucking until her knees buckled.

"Stash, we were going to . . . We can't, not again."

Words were one thing, but Stash knew body language, and hers was saying something altogether different.

"It's late. Danny and Shelly will be back."

He crossed to the door with three short strides and locked it. Something about that click and the mutinous look in his eyes made Mariah go very still inside.

"Let them break it down," he said. "You and I are not finished."

And wouldn't be until she danced with him, and loved him, and slept with him again.

Morning. Birds and open windows. Sounds of the camp waking up, alarms ringing far off. A comfortable sagging mattress. Mariah, too sleepy to stretch, took a languid tour of her body. Legs on the verge of being shaky, skin everywhere softly abraded by contact with other skin, other sweat. Neck peppered with kisses and ears still humming with whispers and dark words. And other places, warm, wet, and worn out.

And her mouth. Oh, yes. Mariah felt hers curve in a smile at the thought of last night. Dancing and making love. The two were definitely linked, permanently entwined. More images and sense memories seeped into the bed with her.

The shower was running. Shelly must be up early. But—"Wait a minute!"

She sat up straight, remembering at the last moment to clutch the sheet to her breasts. Looking around wide-eyed, she swiped a handful of hair out of her eyes. "Stash?"

Her call was answered by a muffled voice in the bathroom. The water turned off. "Are you awake?" he asked.

She could hear his grin. "You were supposed to wake me! Where's Danny? What will Shelly think? Where're my jeans, darn it?" Mariah was stepping from the bed when the door burst open and Danny entered with an armful of fast-food bags. She jumped back under the covers.

"New York Deli delivery! 'Morning, love."

"Never mind," she muttered. "Here's Danny." Her dancers never, underline never, found her in bed with other company members. This was terrible. The fact that Danny had to remove her clothes from one of the dinette chairs made it worse.

"I thought you two were up," he said. "Heard voices coming around the corner."

"We're awake," Mariah admitted grudgingly.

"Ah. There's a robe for you," Stash said, calmly stepping from the bathroom. A thick fluffy towel covered all of him that needed to be covered. He ran a hand through his wet hair. "There." He lifted his brows and indicated a black silk robe, then wandered back into the bathroom. A blow dryer began its whine.

Danny was busy doling out coffee in paper cups and containers of what smelled suspiciously like fresh hot flapjacks. Her stomach winning out over her badly dented sense of propriety, Mariah slipped into the robe while his back was turned.

By the time Danny had offered her his chair, dragged up a spare third, and lit his first cigarette of the day, Mariah had a mouthful of thick, hot syrupy pancake. She was famished.

"Not allowed," she chided Danny, waving away the plume of smoke.

"You turning me in, chief?"

"I could never understand dancers smoking."

"Worse things can happen. Sprains, tendinitis. This way I choose my poison."

Mariah watched the cream swirl in her coffee, his words echoing in her mind. "Does Stash ever complain?"

"About his knee or my smoking? Nah. He's

managing. Up a couple times a night stretching, that's all."

"Thanks for telling me."

Danny shrugged again. Darkly handsome in a lean, elongated way, he had a casual, friendly manner that could put anyone at ease. He'd had his work cut out for him at the moment, she thought.

"I haven't had much chance to talk to you since we got here," she said.

"Since Stash joined us, you mean. Well, you've been busy."

"Not doing this," she rushed in, waving a hand toward the bed.

His brows rose and a grin broke free. "No one said you had."

"Except every newspaper in New York."

Another shrug. "These things take time."

And what exactly were these "things"? she wondered. An affair? An arrangement? A dreaded one-night stand? "I'm sorry if we locked you out. Where did you sleep?"

"Your place."

Mariah swallowed her pancake with a gulp. "With Shelly?"

Danny waved his cigarette in self-defense. "Didn't lay a hand on her, promise. Twin beds. Like here."

Mariah glanced over her shoulder at one decidedly rumpled bed and its neat and tidy mate. The flapjack did a flip-flop in her stomach. "Danny . . ."

"Want to hear some juicy gossip?"

"Only if it's not about me and Stash."

"Don't tell me that's just gossip."

"Not anymore. What's your story?" Maybe it would take her mind off her embarrassment. Although heaven knows, Danny acted as if there was nothing untoward at all about her being there at seven o'clock in the morning. She blinked the grit out of her eyes.

"You know all that trouble you've been having with Shelly?" he said.

"She has a crush on Stash."

"Uh-uh. Me." He proudly pointed the cigarette at his chest. "She's crazy about me and very upset I haven't noticed."

"But you're—"

"I know—'morning, Stash—I'm gay."

Coming up behind her, Stash touched Mariah's neck. She turned instantly. A wave of soap-scented air wafted after him. He kissed her lightly, then reached around her for a cup of coffee as he slid into a chair. "Good morning, all."

Mariah tried to be casual, but with a towel draped around his bare shoulders, wearing no more than black sweat pants with his name in pink script embroidered along the pocket, Stash was more tempting than the food. The black hairs sprinkled across his chest glistened wetly in the sunshine.

"Marvelous breakfast, Dan," he said, eyeing the food eagerly. "You're a chef and caterer both."

"Fits the stereotype."

Stash's innocent expression would have done an altar boy proud. "What stereotype is that?"

Danny gave a bark of laughter. "Maybe male dancers don't get this where you come from. As it is, I'm expected to be good with food, clothes, and dancing." He cocked his wrist in a Bette Davis pose and puffed his cigarette. "You, my friend, are completely at the other end of the spectrum, so don't worry."

Both men laughed. Stash reached for Mariah's hand under the table and squeezed it gently. "So why is she frowning like this?"

"Pour that woman some coffee," Danny advised. "She's always like this on the road. Needs a caffeine jump start every day of her life."

Stash complied.

It looked scalding, but Mariah gulped it down. Her head was whirling like an out of control meteorite, bouncing off planets named Stash, Danny, Shelly. But the planet with the greatest gravitational pull was Stash. She was still holding his hand. She dragged her attention back to Dan. "What was this about Shelly again?"

"She wanted me to be interested in her and was insulted when I wasn't."

"But how could she not know you're gay?"

"Eternal optimism of youth, I guess."

"You two *have* been close," Mariah murmured, working it out in her head. "She's had that *People* magazine picture of both of you framed. I thought it was because she liked the attention."

"You mean some women like publicity?" Stash asked ingenuously.

Mariah scowled again. "Only the vain ones."

Danny peered into his coffee. "It's not all so innocent. When Stash joined and the press descended, I put my arm around Shelly every time a photographer came by." He paused, then added, "Mom was very pleased I'd finally met someone."

"She doesn't know?"

"Like Shelly, I think she knows but hopes for

'better things.' But no problem. Shel and I talked it out last night and she shouldn't give you any more hassle." He got up to leave. "Off for a swim."

"Thanks for taking it easy with her," Mariah said as he passed.

"She isn't grown-up yet, but she's getting there."

Mariah sighed as the screen door slapped shut behind him. "I know the feeling."

Stash had finished off three pancakes to her one. He brushed a crumb of toast off his lip and kissed her cheek so sweetly, her heart turned over. She wasn't ready for this relationship. How could she have ever thought she was? Not this much, not this public, not this soon. She should have known from watching him dance that where Stash was concerned, nothing proceeded cautiously. One leaped wholeheartedly or not at all.

And if one got injured on the way down? Landed with a bang? Hearts were organs; they couldn't really break, could they?

A horrible "what have I gotten myself into" feeling swept over her. "I must go."

"Mariah."

"I'm teaching a class at nine. Later."

A kiss, a wriggle into her clothes, and she was gone.

Mariah rehearsed her afternoon class in a clearing in the woods. It was a bit unorthodox, but a wooden floor wasn't necessary for the upper body work they were doing. Neither was a mirror at this stage. Sometimes it was better to look inside and see how it felt. That was exactly what she hoped to do with herself.

When class was over, she led the girls, laughing and sun-warmed, into the dance room. "Shhh," she commanded.

The boys were strutting their stuff, showing off the culmination of Stash's afternoon tutoring. Mariah watched. When class broke up, she joined Stash beside the piano. "You're very patient with them."

"They're very good."

"You know, only when you're teaching do I see you take your time."

"*Only* when I'm teaching?" The dark flare in his eyes was meant for her.

"You know what I mean."

His smile was wide and knowing. And a little sad. "And you know what I mean for a change. We communicate better and better, no?"

"Excuse me." A young man stepped between them to grab a tattered dance bag from beneath the piano. "Thanks."

"Why are you smiling?" she whispered to Stash as the boy raced out.

"He reminds me of myself at that age, how careless I was."

"And of Sergei?"

He nodded, a guarded look in his eyes. "Yes. All afternoon I hear the same things coming from my mouth."

"Ever wonder what he'd think to see you teaching what he taught?"

"I try not to," he replied shortly.

Mariah blinked and bit back a pained gasp.

Stash looked at her, snaking his arm around her waist. "Sorry."

"Is something wrong?" If she had been a one-night stand, she'd appreciate knowing before she made a complete fool of herself. But coming right out and asking was another thing entirely.

The worried look in her eye wasn't hard to miss. Stash knew he'd put it there. "I'm tired. I ache. Young people take it out of you." So did loving a woman half the night and wondering all morning if you were good enough for her.

"Were you leaping?" she asked.

"Only to get their attention."

"You had it."

"And how do I win yours?"

Now that they were alone, he touched her lightly, fingers strumming her breast as if it were a balalaika. His smile lit up everything but the circles under his eyes. He reminded her of the woods then, sunlight piercing shadows, cool private spots one hesitated to enter.

"That air of mystery is appealing," she whispered.

"Ah, then, it works. I'll have to try it again sometime."

She laughed against his neck, the shadows gone. How could she not love this man? She hugged him.

"You Americans are so open with your feelings. It's nice."

"And Russians aren't? You're the one who goes all out."

"Not in all things. Living in that society taught me to keep many things hidden."

Like dissatisfaction, she thought with a shiver. Was he hinting this wasn't all he wanted? Could it be over so soon? They'd had one night together.

And when morning had come, she had run out on him as fast as she could.

Had she hurt him? Was he doubting too? How callous of her to think only of her own confusion. She'd never seen the doubts in his eyes. He'd never let her see them.

The word *lonely* sprang into her head. She should have seen it before now. No one moved that hard and fast, kept so many plates spinning at once, unless he was afraid of being alone.

"Will you have dinner with me?" he asked.

"Where?"

"We return to the cabin and decide."

The twinkle in his eye started a tingling in her calves that worked its way up her body. "Is that all we're going to do there?"

"We could make love."

That bluntly.

"What is it?" he asked.

"You just come right out and say it," she said. "Is it so simple for you?" *Or do you need me that much?*

"Is not always simple." He touched her face. "We've been apart eight hours. You're cheeks are red, there's a sprinkling of perspiration between your breasts. I want to kiss it away and bring it back again. I missed you."

Moving fast as always. Mariah should have been ready for it. She could be as long as she was honest with herself, and with him.

Nine

They walked side by side down the dirt path, talking about dance and students, while Mariah wondered how to broach the subject of closeness. Genuine closeness took time. Unlike choreography, she couldn't simply demand he show her the emotions she needed to see.

And yet, he was showing her many things. Touching, teasing, running his fingers along the back of her neck as they neared the cabin. Blurring her thoughts, stirring her sensations. Something as subtle as the pulse at the side of his jaw, the sound of his breathing, sent a tingle racing over her skin.

They entered the sparsely furnished room. The smell of logs and linoleum mingled with the tang of pine and sex and, faintly, of Danny's cigarettes. They read the note he'd left on the table and knew they had until suppertime.

She'd donned a sweater to ward off a chill. Stash peeled it away, making her conscious of the soft give of knitted buttonholes. The leotard was next. Then the lock on the cabin door.

She'd missed him. One touch and she luxuriated in the feel of his body against hers. All the emotions she'd learned to express onstage but never share in private, never like this, rose within her. It was a kind of strength. As much as he needed, she could give.

Music from the open-air auditorium rumbled through the window. Stash swayed slowly. "This is one dance we haven't done."

Made-up steps, motions for a stage of their own. "You like this dance?" he asked.

"I need to see it in front of an audience," she said coyly.

"Hard to see if you're in it."

"Yes, but the audience reacts."

"You could watch on TV. You could tape us rehearsing."

"Yes."

"Or watch in mirrors."

"Mirrors," she murmured.

Another heat started slowly, her imagination wired to the shimmering sensations sweeping her body.

"Some people put them over the bed," he said, "in this decadent country of yours, or so I've heard."

"Kind of kinky."

"And exciting. Nothing wrong with that."

"Nothing at all," she agreed, her voice throaty and low.

They fumbled with clothes until, body to body, he stood her against him.

She wanted his kisses but wasn't at all sure she

could deal with his steely gaze. He watched the way her nipples hardened, the way her limbs shook. Maybe he couldn't see that, but he had to feel it when he parted her thighs with his knee.

"Are you watching, Mariah?" His voice was smooth as music, husky as a saxophone.

Head bowed, she saw her hand join his to smooth on the protection he'd reached for. Stepping between her legs, he slowly rose and entered her.

Her arms held tight around his neck as he guided her legs around his waist. "This is a dance," he breathed. "Open your eyes, Mariah, and see."

Although her lids were heavy, she did so, staring into the turbulent darkness of his as he moved within her, danced inside her, made her tense and weak at the same time, like paper curling and wilting in the flames, lifted up by the fire itself, then higher, then released into sparks and flares and the hiss of a heat wave.

"Oh my." She rested her head against his neck.

He bent to sit her on the bed, watching her arch back. But her hands were still locked around his neck and she wasn't letting him go that easily.

"Where do you think you're going?" she murmured.

"This was for you. I wanted to show you—to thank you—" There were so many things he wanted to tell her. That he loved her was only one, and it was the easiest to show, the hardest to say.

She smiled, lazy and wondrous, shaking her head from side to side in a determined no. The pout of her lips should have warned him right there. "You watched while I did all that myself."

"I helped."

"It's your turn."

"Mariah."

"Come here, you."

There was only so much a man could resist. Mariah with a satisfied smile on her lips wasn't one of them.

He sank willingly beside her.

"Uh-uh." She wasn't having it. She crooked a knee beside his hip and made it clear she planned to give as good as she got. "In my lessons on the birds and the bees, you go here, I believe."

So he did. And it wasn't surprising that words failed him. Her hands touched either side of his face as she took control, making him open his eyes, guiding his mouth to hers. "Stash."

It was the way her mouth formed his name. The S in Stash, her even white teeth biting off the T, the pout that ended it all in a long *shhh*. There were only so many demands a woman could make on a man's willpower, and Mariah was a demanding woman.

"Watch," she commanded. Her lips liked that word too. "Watch what you do to me."

He would. As soon as his arms stopped shaking while he held his chest off hers. Her breasts rose and fell, their crests just touching him as her hands brazenly traveled down his chest.

He stiffened and cried out, freezing exactly where he was.

She smiled.

He didn't move. A pale line of tension formed around his mouth.

"Stash?"

It took a moment before her voice penetrated the

pain. He managed to roll over on his back. "Sorry." He could barely get the word out.

"What's wrong?" Heart pumping in overtime, Mariah was on her knees beside him. "What is it?"

"Cramp."

It was that all right. She saw the knot that made him raise one knee. The back of his thigh felt like petrified wood.

"Hamstring," she said.

He reeled off half a dozen Russian words that weren't quite so anatomical.

"Just lie still."

There wasn't a lot else he could do. He listened to the clatter of Mariah flinging things out of the medicine cabinet.

"Some liniment might help." She twisted off the cap. It was a thoroughly unromantic smell, medicinal and sinus-clearing. Her massage didn't do much good. "It's like rubbing a knotted rope. Try to relax, breathe into it."

That helped. Stash looked up at her, fury at his helplessness flashing in his eyes. Then they snapped shut as he grimaced in pain.

"It was better," she said. "Relax again if you can."

"It's not so easy," he replied, reaching up to close the lapels of the silk robe she'd tossed on. With thumb and forefinger he tugged it together, stretching it over breasts it wasn't designed to hide. One long finger traced her breastbone, down into the cleft.

"Maybe it's a sign," he muttered. "About my dancing."

"Phooey. I've had these off and on all my life. You should have stretched longer after class."

"I was stretched to the max a minute ago."

She grinned. "Your English gets better all the time."

"Thanks to you." He struggled to sit up.

Her palm tingled from liniment as she pushed him back. "Stay there."

He clamped that hand to his chest. "I don't want you to love me." Stash knew from her confused, humored look that she thought his English was failing him again. Maybe she thought he was speaking of tender loving care. He didn't deserve that either.

"I think it's a little late for that," she retorted lightly. She stretched into her leotard and pulled up her jeans.

She was smooth and sleek, yet rounded and full at the same time. Her hair was mussed and her face flushed. The low front of the leotard showed him how far that flush went. The look in her eyes told him even more.

He didn't want her loving him.

He listened to water running as she washed her hands, thinking of the headlines that became more of a challenge every day, daring him to call New York and see about the possibility of returning to the USSR.

And his love for Mariah only got deeper.

He sat up. "Mariah, I want to talk to you."

Standing in the bathroom doorway drying her hands, she could see he had something on his mind. The frown was definitely back. He'd been brooding and doubting and fighting some demon since she'd walked in on his rehearsals.

Perhaps the young men he'd been working with had made him think too much of careers, their beginnings and endings. Getting a cramp at the worst possible time couldn't have helped. A little ego-massaging was needed. "You'd make a wonderful coach," she said. "Those boys idolize you. Their romantic defector."

"Is it romantic to be a traitor?" He had to find a way to convince her he was not the man for her.

She perched on the opposite bed. "Want to talk about it?"

"The story is known everywhere." A disgusted wave of his hand indicated the entire world. "I betrayed my family. Is that the kind of man you want to love? Someone who would leave his closest friends behind?"

"Can't you call them?"

"The phones are tapped. They'd be in contact with a known traitor." He plucked at the white nubs of the bedspread.

"Perhaps they could escape too."

"Because of me they're watched."

She touched his hand. "It must be hard for you."

"Harder for them."

As with his knee, she realized, he wouldn't impose this pain on her.

The leg still wasn't good; he bounced it restlessly. He threw an arm over his head and looked up at the ceiling. "My sister wanted to be a scientist. She ended up a schoolteacher in a miserable little town. My mother is in one squabble after another with the government, petty harassment. I succeed and they pay for it. It isn't right."

The joyful crash of a cymbal echoed from the auditorium as the symphony rehearsal came to a close. Stash and Mariah listened for a moment.

"It isn't your fault."

"No?" The woman was too much. He'd left his

family to an uncertain fate and she defended him.

"You were ten years ahead of your time, Stash. Look at all the people protesting the system now. For all you know, your actions might have spurred some of them on, shown them there was another way."

"But they stayed to fight. I ran away."

"Bullwinkle." Her eyes flashed, passionate with feeling.

"You'd carry a banner, Mariah. I see the fire in your eyes. You'd march, not run like a coward, thinking only of your career."

"Coward?" she replied in astonishment. "Defecting takes courage. What would have happened if you'd gotten caught?"

He shrugged. "I lose my position as dancer. Go to prison or internal exile."

"Siberia, you mean."

He gestured as if that were nothing.

"You won't convince me that defecting isn't brave."

He had to. It was important that she see what he lived with, what he was. "I left my family, Mariah."

He wanted to reach across the space between the beds and take her hand. He swung his legs off the other side instead. Standing gingerly, he limped to the window and looked out at the lake. It glittered through the trees like New York harbor had the day his plane landed in America. His first day as a free man. But he'd never be truly free unless he faced the past.

"I leave everyone, Mariah. That's what you should know about me. I've been called a selfish egotist and a traitor."

"The people who said those things didn't know—

didn't love you," she amended. Time to lay all their cards on the table,

"I'm not a man to love."

"Too late," she whispered, coming up beside him.

Stash grasped her face between his hands. It was so delicate, her skin like pearls, her red hair falling in fine wisps around it. She was a treasure, the kind he couldn't be entrusted with. "People have loved me. They learned."

"And if I choose to believe in the man I love?"

"I tell you—"

"You joined The Movement, remember? A company for people who defy other people's labels."

His brave Mariah, daring Mariah. He took her chin in his hand. "I advise against it, Marishka. I'm telling you I'm not the faithful kind."

He was as loyal as they came, she thought. And the longer she knew him, the more deeply she believed that. "I disagree."

"At your peril."

"Let me decide that."

"American women. Bah." He tried stalking around the room, but his leg was stubborn and stiff. "I'm not the type to stay when I'm unhappy."

"I never said I wanted you to."

"You deserve a better man."

Mariah knew without a doubt she could have another man. She could have just about any safe, sane man she set her sights on. Someone tame, trainable. She'd known coming into this that Stash was different. He *would* leave when his dancing was done. And he might not take her with him. He might not even offer.

She promised herself she could handle it. She

might not be the Swan Queen, but she wasn't a frail little flower either. This was all about loving him while he was there. "You act as if I'm going to crumble if this doesn't last for all eternity."

Stash turned to face her. She had her chin tilted up, her shoulders square. Why was it that when she acted strong and brave, he wanted to protect her even more?

"I love you," she said easily. "But that doesn't mean I'm tying you down. That also means"—she crossed her arms, tapped her foot—"that I refuse to hear a bad word about you, even from you."

"I could give you dozens."

"*Nyet.* No more." She'd learned that cutting motion with the hand pretty well, if she did say so herself. It silenced him completely for ten seconds. "You made a tough decision in impossible circumstances. Forgive yourself."

"And my family? Would they forgive me that simply?"

"How do you know they haven't already? Maybe they were thrilled you'd escaped."

The woman knew entirely too much about love, he thought. That she was right didn't make it easier. In fact, it twisted like a knife. People blinded by love rarely saw what a swine a man one was. "I feel like a foot," he declared disgustedly.

"A what?"

He lifted his leg and pointed. "I'm lower than the bottom of a foot, yes?"

"You mean you're a heel."

"Exactly!"

Mariah couldn't stop her guffaw, couldn't resist the urge to put her arms around him and squeeze.

"Your English goes to hell when you're upset, you know."

"So suit me."

"I think I already do," she murmured, still laughing.

"Was that wrong too?"

"It's either 'shoot me' or 'sue me' and I don't plan on doing either." She'd been right to recognize the loneliness in him. "You haven't seen your mother or sister for ten years?"

"No, but they've seen me."

A light dawned, more like a flashbulb. "That's why you court the paparazzi."

"Yes."

To think she'd thought him vain. She wondered for a instant what his mother would think when she saw them together. "Kind of like what Danny was talking about this morning. Sending messages through the press."

He nodded. "I wanted her to see you."

For a man who insisted she not love him, he wasn't making it easy. "Couldn't you go back sometime? Things have eased up so much recently."

"And could go bad just as fast. I must dance."

"New York will keep you busy."

"Not too busy for us, I hope."

"If Janine's phone calls are any indication, we won't have much free time. We have six more weeks here, and when we get back, there'll be only one month till the premiere. I have so much work to do with the ensemble."

"You'll stay at my apartment," he decided instantly.

She planted a kiss on the nose of her benevolent dictator. "Sorry, but I have my own."

"In Brooklyn!"

"It's not Siberia."

"If you don't come, we'll end up living by appointment."

"Look who's talking. You're the one with commitments up the wazoo."

He shook his head. "My only commitments are in New York City."

She blinked. "Wazoo isn't a place, it's— Oh, never mind. You have so many business interests to catch up on, I might not see you until the premiere itself."

"I'll dance with you every night." He touched her, then held her, then kissed her. "One way or the other."

He'd give her all he could, he promised himself. Loving Mariah, like living, like dancing, would be as intense as he could make it. Endings were inevitable. This time he wanted no regrets. The woman was going to be lavished with love. Or was the word *ravished*?

Closed up for the months of June and July, Mariah's apartment was as stuffy as a recently discovered pyramid tomb. August air didn't promise to make it any better. She opened her windows to traffic and a whiff of garbage. "New York, New York," she hummed.

The mail was in a pile, the plants were dusty but alive. The only color and life in the place was the dozen roses.

Stash. She remembered the flashbulbs at the airport, the presentation of the flowers, the publicity. He treated her like the world's greatest ballerina. She smiled at the roundabout way this ugly duckling had gotten there.

Of course, all anyone was interested in was their love affair. "No comments" were pointless. She was sure her feelings showed. If her reflection in the bathroom mirror was any indication, she practically radiated.

Practicing a few tart "no comments" anyway, she started a bath. The water ran brown for the first thirty seconds.

It would take a while to get up to New York speed, the dash and pace of the place. According to Constanza and Janine, rehearsals of the rest of the company had been desultory but regularly attended. She had one month to whip them into shape, a month in which it would be absolutely impossible to get any work done if she moved in with Stash as he requested.

Before stepping into the tepid water, she brought his roses in and set them on the counter. Lord, she loved that man. How on earth was she expected to stay away from him?

Reporters clogged the hall, and photographers were clumped in the doorway of the rehearsal room. Hearing Constanza's voice, Mariah wrapped up the interview in her office. Time to take control of this situation on day one, she thought. A short speech, an offer to allow pictures for limited time periods, then the company was off-limits. Mariah was taking control. It felt good.

"Out!" she called as she strode down the hall. "Everybody out. Rehearsal begins in five minutes." Stash, in the back of the rehearsal room with the tightest knot of people around him, thanked her with a glance but continued to play affable star to her wicked witch while the place cleared out. Knowing his family was the reason behind the high profile, she didn't mind at all.

She signaled Janine and the music began. "We have four main numbers worked out already, solos for Stash, Danny, and Shelly. The four group numbers are variations on these. I've tried to work them out in my head as much as possible. But you know me, I've got to see before I know it's right."

Stash caught her eye. She suppressed a grin as she cleared her throat. "Any questions?"

He watched her go through the first routine. Did she know how happy she looked? This was her company—the work, the headaches, the constant commands to express more. She was home. Having given his up, he envied her. And loved her. And knew he'd miss her if the plans his manager had hinted at the previous evening came true.

"We may have an opening; be ready to jump," he'd said. "Plane to Paris, Berlin, then Moscow."

"When?" Stash had asked, the blood in his veins feeling cool, thin.

"That's the million-dollar question."

Stash only hoped he'd have time to warn Mariah.

After a life of jumping, he thought he'd found a place to land. But not for long. Never for long.

Mariah worked the dancers hard, trying not to lavish all her attention on Stash. But flashes of skin inside that torn T-shirt kept distracting her. Shivering, she had to clear her voice again. "Stash, will you go through this with me, please? I want to demonstrate our pas de deux so they can see how the lines develop."

"Certainly." He walked forward, stopping a little too close. He bowed his head with a sharp nod.

Mariah's hand was halfway to his forehead before she stopped herself from smoothing back his hair. Their music began.

Ten

You Don't Send Me Flowers. Not true. He sent them every other day.

Did he sing her love songs? Yes, if she counted his soft humming while they danced, the lowness of his voice communicating only to her, making breathlike ripples shimmy on her skin.

He bent her back, but she slipped out of his embrace and walked away. She returned. Stash knew he should be the one dancing the part about leaving, but this wasn't the time for talk.

They danced for the other dancers. No denials, no rumors. Their love was as clear as the image in the mirror, heads bowed, torsos leaning, arms reaching, but in opposite directions. It was a visual ache, but the love was undeniable.

It finished. The applause of the other dancers almost drowned out the brisk knock on the door.

A man in a suit and tie barged in, his highly polished street shoes drumming on the wooden floor. He didn't even say Stash's name. One look, and Stash's face darkened. "Excuse me, Mariah."

She felt inexplicably naked when he let her go, as if his body had been a shield. She tried not to shiver. The sudden hollow feeling in her stomach was silly and irritating. The man acted like he owned Stash. Just another claim on his attention.

She crossed her arms and swiftly turned to her dancers. "Well, looks like we can't keep them all out, can we? Janine, new music?"

Variations on patterns with Shelly and Danny. It was difficult to lead her dancers while glancing over her shoulder every few seconds at the two men talking, their heads close together.

Then the stranger, his voice low and urgent, put a hand on Stash's back and steered him toward the door.

Mariah had had enough. "Excuse me, people. Stash!"

Her voice sounded sharp in the uncarpeted hallway as she strode after them. The door to the rehearsal room swung shut, hushing the music behind her.

The quick, guarded look Stash gave her before ducking into the men's dressing room was all her heart needed to go into a free-fall.

She turned to the other man. "What, may I ask, is going on here?"

"Mitchell Conway, Stash's manager." He shot a cuff and extended his hand.

"Mariah Heath."

"It's about time we met." Conway's hand was as smooth as his manner, his haircut, his suit. It figured.

"Mr. Conway, we're rehearsing. I've made it clear to everyone involved that outside interests will have to wait until lunch or breaks."

"It's a little late for that."

Before she could ask what he meant, Stash appeared in the doorway of the dressing room, his leather coat slung over his shoulders, an impatient, brooding look on his face.

That look stopped Mariah cold.

"I'm ready," he said to Conway. "We go."

He strode briskly down the hall, with no intention of looking back. It was hard enough leaving.

Mariah whispered his name. That was all it took. He turned.

Three days later, that whisper called everything back for her, like a movie, a memory on constant replay.

She should have yelled, screamed, run after him, demanded how he could simply walk away as if he had more important business elsewhere. Instead, she'd said his name, and he'd turned.

Pacing outside the office of Mitchell Conway, she remembered the look on his face, and the more startled expression on Conway's. He'd quickly reappraised the situation, and she'd realized he'd never seen Stash in love.

At the same moment she'd understood that she might never see Stash again. "What's going on?" she'd asked. "Where are you going? We have rehearsals." The words weren't enough. They sounded petty and angry. But what other words were there?

Stash walked back to her slowly, the coat swaying on his shoulders, releasing the smell of leather. He touched her face, "My love." The gravity of the gesture made her catch her breath. "I have no words for this."

The word good-bye echoed in her head. She couldn't suggest it, couldn't dream it.

He didn't say it.

Conway loomed behind him. "We've got to go, Stash."

The abyss widened with every step he took backward.

"My family—" he said. "I will contact you."

Contact, she thought dully, still feeling the palm on her cheek.

He was going. She watched the set of his shoulders, the coat heavy on them.

He'd never actually said it, a part of her insisted. So why was good-bye the only word she heard?

Three days later, rumors flying, she'd come to Conway for answers.

Stash was injured. She'd laughed at the first headline. It was exactly what he'd said they'd say if she barred the press.

Stash went to Paris.

He's making a movie.

He's in Betty Ford.

They had a lover's spat.

He went back to Russia.

And surprise of surprises, he had.

"He wouldn't go without telling me," Mariah insisted to Conway.

"He had to."

She paced around the gray and black office of Mitchell Conway, forty stories up in the multinational management firm of Icanthus, Conway, and

Stern. The man was only slightly less remote than the decor.

"You love him," he said, his voice low and confidential.

She stopped pacing. "More important, he loves me, and you know it."

Conway glanced down at his desk, obviously surprised she had caught his look in the hallway. The man wasn't used to giving things away. "I've known Stash since he landed in this country."

A smooth change of subject, but Mariah fell for it. "And? Are you telling me I've been duped? Just another thrown-over conquest of the notorious Stashkolnikov?"

Conway leaned back in a leather chair designed to impress.

Mariah stared him down. He blinked first.

Reaching across his expansive desk, without a scrap of paper marring the mirrorlike surface, Conway picked up a gold pen and turned it end over end in his hands. "His reputation speaks for itself, don't you think?"

"His reputation doesn't mean diddly here. We both know him better than that. He's loyal to those he loves."

Conway halted the beginning of a smile, pulling his mouth back into a noncommittal line. "More so than you may know," he murmured. "If it's any consolation, I believe he does love you."

"I'm not here for consolation. I have to know what's going on! The press sharks have been circling rehearsals all week, not to mention my apartment stairs."

"You're under pressure and persistent questioning."

"You said it." And she ached for Stash. That was harder to say.

"Then the less you know the better." Conway sprang into action, snagging a business card out of a marble holder. "Refer all press contacts to his management. We'll handle everything."

"Mr. Conway, I'm perfectly capable of managing my own affairs." She grimaced at that last word.

"To tell you the truth, Ms. Heath, it was Stash's request that you be taken care of."

Anger flared in her eyes. "I am not some floozy looking for financial support."

It was Conway's turn to flinch. "Perhaps I misspoke."

She stalked around the office, which this man had obviously earned. "Won't someone please give me a simple answer? Stash said something about his family. You act like this is a State Department secret."

"It is."

"Then it's true. He is in Russia." Where else would he go that was more important than the two of them?

"You mustn't confirm or deny this to anyone."

"I need to know."

Conway thought it over. She could tell he wasn't a man to betray confidences easily. She seldom asked anyone to. Honesty, that was all she asked. And sometimes even those you loved couldn't provide it. A too-familiar stab of pain stopped her in her tracks.

He'd barely looked back.

He hadn't said good-bye.

Conway's voice broke into her thoughts. "He had a chance to go back, secretly. If he'd gone publicly, the Soviet government would have expected him to dance. A refusal would have been seen as a snub. "This trip is strictly personal. We wanted it all very low-profile. Unfortunately, that's a little hard to manage with Stash."

Didn't she know it. "But he'll come back. I mean, they can't make him stay. There'd be an uproar."

Conway turned the pen over one more time. "He might choose to stay."

The silence started forty stories below and rose like a numbing fog. Words rushed in to fill it. Stash's words, all his warnings about defecting, about how she shouldn't trust the kind of man who would defect. He'd warned her and she hadn't listened.

Someone had brought in a tray. Conway poured the coffee.

Mariah pulled her shoulders back. With effort she raised her chin. Dancing had taught her posture. Hers, at the moment, was impeccable. As precise and perfect as the contracts drawn up in this office.

An idea crept up on her like the street noise below. "Mr. Conway."

"Yes, Miss Heath?" He poured the cream.

"We have a contract."

The words hung there, like the sugar cube he held suspended in a pair of silver tongs. "And?"

"I expect it to be honored."

He offered her a cup. She shook her head. Leaning back, balancing the saucer in one hand while he plucked absently at the crease in his slacks, Stash's manager took a deep breath. "These circumstances were totally unforeseen when the contract was drawn up. Events in the Soviet Union have been so precipitous—"

"If you're going to claim force majeure, keep it. What happens in Russia is their business. Stash's actions, despite his considerable ego, do not constitute an act of God."

Even Conway chuckled at that.

"Besides," Mariah continued, "as you yourself implied, something like this doesn't happen overnight. There must have been a lot of groundwork done. You'd have to clear it with the State Department. The Soviets too."

And all this had been going on while he was dancing with her, loving her, speaking softly in the dark. He hadn't told her, hadn't let her in that last guarded part of him. That hurt even more.

Conway pursed his lips to blow on his coffee. "It was *way* behind the scenes. We didn't bring Stash in until the plans were set. He couldn't work with something like this hanging over his head. Believe me, we had no inkling this would open up as fast as it has. The situation is very volatile."

"Not as volatile as my lawyer will be when and if your client refuses to honor his contract. We have approximately eighteen days until the premiere, and I expect him there. Or else!"

She walked out, legs shaking, blouse sticking to her back, palms damp. The elevator was walled in marble. As heavy and silent, Mariah thought, as her heart. And as cold. She leaned her cheek against the smooth wall.

He'd tried to warn her.

He'd never promised anything.

Except for the contract: That was the only promise Stash had ever made her. "Like an arranged marriage," he'd said. "We sign a contract."

It would have been funny if tears weren't trickling down her face.

"Turn on *Nightline*!" Janine shouted.

Mariah heard the words before her hand was around the receiver. She pulled a handful of folders off the dusty TV in the corner cabinet while Danny pressed buttons on the remote control. The VCR blinked on, then the screen.

"Ballet star Petr Stashkolnikov returned to Paris from Russia this afternoon—" the announcer was saying.

Mariah watched the pictures of him stepping off the plane. How many airports used those portable stairs anymore? she wondered. They were perfect for photo opportunities.

Was this Stash's way of sending *her* a message?

"And with him was his wife."

Next they discussed the drop in the Dow Jones.

Janine was still talking, evaluating the competition. "No makeup, but not bad. Give that girl a whiff of New York and she'll be all over the counter at Bloomie's in no time."

Danny took the phone out of Mariah's hand. She was listening to something else, words about loyalty to family, other commitments. A wife certainly qualified!

"Don't trust me," he'd said.

"Don't worry," she said aloud.

"You okay?"

She looked up at Danny, shell-shocked but calm. The numbness was gone. Anger, steady and growing, had taken its place. "He's married and he's coming back to New York."

"And?"

"And he's going to honor that contract."

She worked through the weekend. If she could have worked through the night and right up to rehearsal time, Mariah would have done it.

They were three weeks into August. Summer hadn't burned itself out yet, but it tried its damnedest that Monday. Fifteen minutes into the morning class and sweat poured off her. Her dancers were about ready to revolt. Like a shark smelling blood, she was after the emotion.

"I know how the step looks, Marcus, I want to see how it *feels*. Do it again."

She turned to walk back to the front of the room just as Stash entered. Their eyes met in the mirror.

Black T-shirt, black slacks of parachute silk, a cover-up for his tights. He strode across the room. Janine stopped playing. The world stopped.

"I'm ready to dance," he said.

Mariah wasn't ready to let him. She whirled to face him and the class.

"Excuse me," she said to the dancers. "Fifteen-minute break."

He followed her down the dismal hall and into the women's dressing room.

She swiftly dragged a brush through her hair, dropped the brush onto the table with a clunk, and twisted her ponytail into a bun that would last a month. A handful of bobbypins scraped her scalp.

One would have thought neatness and control were stand-ins for dignity and fury.

"Will you hear me out?" he asked.

"No." As painful as it was to speak, the shock value was worth it. He was momentarily speechless. Knowing Stash, she suspected he'd been planning some kind of speech all the way there. For the moment, his occasionally skewed English was something she'd rather not deal with. "I understand from your manager that you intend to honor your commitments."

"Mariah."

"All of them."

"Mariah."

"Don't lie to me, Stash. Just please don't lie—" Her voice broke. Traitor. She swallowed.

"I warned you," he began.

"Oh, please! Spare me the 'I told you so.' I made a fool of myself. I was afraid I might. Don't rub it in."

The only thing Stash wanted to rub was the tension in her neck and the back of her shoulders.

"You'll dance, dammit," she said.

"I will."

"Danny can't do every role, and people have paid to see you."

"Then we are agreed."

She turned on him. "Oh, one more thing: You never said a truer word than when you said you betrayed the people you loved."

With her back against the makeup table and him between her and the door, she couldn't just march past him. She supposed it was his turn to speak anyhow. As long as she held on to her dignity, her posture, and the edge of the table, she'd make it. "Well?"

"When I go, I go. I don't look back." That was his credo, and yet, he hadn't stopped thinking about her since he'd left her. Even in Russia there hadn't been an hour when he hadn't thought of her. "Mariah."

She turned away, glancing in the mirror, not seeing anything but the man behind her shoulder. He was reaching for her. She slid past him and headed for the door.

It was her turn not to look back.

But Stash knew he could make her turn with one short phrase. He used it. "She's not my wife, Mariah."

Eleven

Mariah stopped, though she didn't face him.

"She's my sister," he went on. "The press got it wrong. It wasn't something I wanted to explain on the phone. I thought you'd be hurt." He never realized she'd be cold.

"Is that it?" she asked.

"I had to go back and get them out while I could." She turned at that.

"Your mother came too?"

"My mother refused."

His voice was so low, she wasn't sure she'd heard correctly. The dark and simmering look on his face confirmed it, though.

"Why?" she asked.

He made a cutting gesture with his hand as if it were beyond thinking. "She says she knows no other life. And Tatiana—"

"Tatiana came with you."

"Already she's threatening to go back. She misses her fiancé."

Mariah's brows rose.

"He's involved with the new politics," Stash added.

"Good for him."

"It's dangerous."

"And Tatiana?"

"She says she wants to be with him."

"Good for her."

Stalking around the room, Stash threw his arm out to the side as if flinging off any opposition. "It could change overnight, Mariah! I want her safe. Here. My mother is being stubborn, like when she sent me away to dance when I was a child. Or when I defected. How can a mother be happy to see her son go?"

"Only if she loves him so much she puts his happiness above hers."

He ran a hand through his hair, his shoulders sagging. His eyes were dark with despair, his voice harsh and guttural. "And how does he repay her, Mariah? Tell me that."

All the anger she'd cultivated was suddenly swallowed up in an aching void. She was going to lose him, and there was no way she could hate him for it or even blame him. Of course he wouldn't leave his family behind. She wouldn't love a man who was capable of that.

"You pretended you'd turned your back on your past," she said, "but you've planned on saving them all along."

"Hoped, Mariah. And waited a long time."

"But they didn't know." Like herself, she thought. A lot of people had been left in the dark as to his plans.

"I couldn't explain it to them. So much depended

on secrecy." He looked at her long and hard, that look he'd given her in the hallway before he left. "When it happened, there wasn't time to explain." He approached her slowly. "I wanted to bring them here to meet the woman I love."

She closed her eyes. Why did it hurt so much to hear it now? An ache welled up inside her, catching in her throat. He said, "I love you." He didn't say he'd stay. "What are you going to do?"

"Go back."

The two words tore at her heart like hooks.

"Until they are safe, Mariah."

She wanted to say something flippant, something about not letting them walk down the streets of New York then, or never letting them out of his sight; but the words wouldn't come. She turned away, hugging herself. She hadn't noticed the surge of hope until it died, whispering at her feet like a discarded costume, lace and chiffon and dreams that weren't going to come true. "That leaves us where we were, doesn't it?"

"I never promised."

"I know."

"I tried, Mariah."

To do what? she wanted to ask him. To treat her like the most special woman on earth? To leave her without hurting her? That had to be it. No one touching her this gently could ever intend to hurt her.

"I could have put Tatiana on the plane and stayed behind."

"Why didn't you?" The words almost didn't make it out. Say it, please say it, her heart cried—

"I had to come back."

—and tore a little bit more.

"Because of the contract, right?" That made him let go. "You had to honor this commitment too." Her eyes pinned him, sparkling with unshed tears, daring him to deny it.

Stash looked away. Every name he'd ever been called echoed through him. Traitor, betrayer. He'd wanted Mariah, to dance with, to love, to fill a void in his life. And she'd given him all that. He owed her every bit as much as he owed his family, if not more. "You are stronger than I when it comes to emotions, Mariah. You don't need secrecy. You have your company, your work. You will survive."

Survival wasn't living, she thought. It wasn't the flowering burst of energy she felt every time he touched her, every time he walked into a room. "Don't you dare tell me I can manage on my own! All these people are not you."

"At least you're safe."

A sudden coldness enveloped her. Her pain wasn't the only thing that mattered here. There were other people involved. "It would be so much easier if I could hate you."

He took her in his arms at last. "Mariah." He tucked her head beneath his chin, feeling the weight of her against his chest. "Mariah."

He'd come back for this. Just to hold her once more. "If hating me makes it easier . . ."

"No, no."

He kissed her hair, smoothed into the tight chignon at the nape of her neck. He wanted to kiss her there, too, but holding her now was more important. "My love hurt you. I didn't mean that."

She laughed, a choked sound that could have been a sob. "You never say exactly what you mean."

"Let me show you." He kissed the top of her head

again, inhaling the faint fruity scent of her shampoo. It was pain as much as love. Tender, desperate, he didn't know which way to turn. Her taste had haunted him. Her independence challenged him. She'd survive without him, he was sure. But would he? Living in Russia, constantly looking back . . .

His kiss was as gentle as rain. The tip of his tongue tasted the salt of tears on her lips, but tentatively, remaining behind the line. There would be pain if he held her any closer.

"Please," she whispered, opening her mouth to his.

He couldn't. The taste in his own mouth was like ashes. He kissed her cheek instead. "I have to go back."

"When? Now?"

"After the premiere."

She hugged him, held him, imprinting their bodies one to the other. The other women in his life might love him, but she had him now.

"What if your mother won't come?" she asked.

"I stay there until she does."

"And how many years of dancing will you give up trying?"

He knew what she was doing. The woman saw through her dancers like a psychiatrist did her patients, or a mother her children. "So I won't dance."

She was silent for a moment, then said, "I could come."

"What?"

"And dance. The Movement could tour the Soviet Union, what there is left of it."

"Don't joke, Mariah."

"Why not? They're letting in artists all the time."

"I do all this to get my loved ones out, not to have them following me in. You stay here."

Her king of Siam again. But a teasing smile deserted her. Without dancing, what did she have to offer him? It was a naked bribe, and it had failed.

"We may have very little time," he said, swallowing the bitterness of irrevocable choices. He touched her and she clung to him. Their kisses were messy, fast, and unsubtle. Sheer numbers couldn't make up for a separation that could last years. And if she found someone else in the meantime, that separation could last a lifetime. He was gambling so much on her waiting. It hadn't been enough to win her once. When he returned he might have to win her all over again. "I will try, Mariah. I will come back."

"When?"

He had no answer, only his hungry kisses.

Mariah felt more than slightly guilty for having alerted the press to keep Stash busy. She felt even more criminal as she slipped into her bag the videotape she'd made of their rehearsal of "You Don't Send Me Flowers." She had to reach his apartment before he did. She needed a few minutes alone with his sister.

The doorman recognized her. Amazing, she thought. Being the infamous new lover of Stashkolnikov had its advantages. The fast elevator had her stomach plummeting. In minutes she was standing before the door to a corner apartment, leaning on the bell.

A raven-haired beauty answered. The only defect in her exotic face was a slight puffiness beneath her eyes. "Tatiana?" Mariah asked.

The woman nodded but didn't speak.

Mariah realized that not only did she not yet know what she planned to say to this woman, she wasn't even sure she spoke English. "Oh, boy."

The woman inclined her head.

Mariah smiled apologetically, pulling out the videotape. "Your brother . . . I, uh . . . You wouldn't happen to have a VCR, would you?"

Tatiana was silent as she scrutinized Mariah from head to foot.

"TV," Mariah said, knowing it was a nearly universal word. "Stash sent me." She spoke the white lie slowly and distinctly. "To watch this with you."

"I see," Tatiana replied.

Obviously her English wasn't much, but she did step back from the door.

Mariah slipped inside. Stash's sister wasn't as helpless, sad, or young as Mariah had expected. Stash had talked about her as if she were a vulnerable child, barely more than Shelly's age. Indicating the sofa with a polite motion of her hand, Tatiana looked more like a mature twenty-five. If she missed her fiancé, it certainly wasn't out of puppy love.

"TV?" Mariah asked.

Tatiana nodded toward a teakwood cabinet. Mariah slid back the doors to reveal a state of the art television and VCR. She found the remote control, inserted the tape, and pressed the necessary buttons.

The VCR whirred on; the music began.

She watched herself dancing with Stash. They moved beautifully together. It wasn't a matter of ego, it was survival. But no, it was more than that. She could survive on her own. She needed Stash to live.

The dance ended and Tatiana picked up the remote control from the coffee table and flicked the off switch.

How quickly they learn, Mariah thought wryly, searching for a way to put into words what that tape so eloquently expressed. She began simply. "I love your brother."

"I see."

Wondering if those were the only two words Tatiana knew, Mariah trudged on. "I love him very much." For the first time she had a sense of what Stash went through trying to make himself understood.

"I *love* him." She hugged herself.

"I love him too," Tatiana replied slowly.

"Oh. Good. Great." What next? One word at a time. "I'm, that is, I am trying to explain why I want him here. Here." She pointed to the carpet.

Tatiana looked at the coffee table.

"No." Mariah wiped that away with a motion of her hand. "Here in New York. I want him to stay."

"Yes?"

"Yes."

The women looked at each other for a moment.

"You would, perhaps, like some coffee?" Tatiana asked, a glimmer of humor in her eyes.

Mariah felt a smile forming on her own face. "You speak English."

"Quite well. Although Stash insists my colloquialisms need work."

Mariah's smile deepened. "Stash has a lot of ideas on how others should behave."

Tatiana laughed. "You've learned that so far. You must love him very much."

That simple phrase. Mariah leaned back against the butter-soft leather of the beige sofa. "I do, Tatiana. But I don't want to tear him away from his family."

Tears filled her eyes again. Mariah fought them while she glanced around for a tissue. Tatiana handed her a hankie.

"I never leave home without one," she said, smiling.

Mariah dabbed at her eyes and indicated the television. "You've been watching a lot of this."

"But this is the first time I see my brother dance since I was child. Thank you." She touched Mariah's hand for a moment, then headed for the kitchen and the coffee. "I didn't know how much I would need that."

Mariah realized she was talking about the handkerchief, not the dancing. "Your fiancé," she said, following Tatiana.

"Ivan Andreyovich."

"You miss him."

"Oh, yes. My eyes have been as red as yours. You take sugar?"

Mariah nodded, considering the incongruity of a samovar in the spartan New York kitchen. The espresso machine fit in better with the modern industrial decor.

"Tatiana, I love Stash. He loves me."

"I hope you don't believe those reports about our being husband and wife. Petr was very upset when he saw them."

Petr? Oh, yes, Petr Ivanovich Stashkolnikov. It was good to know he'd been thinking of her while he'd been away. It warmed her as much as the coffee.

"Vanya said it served him right for leaving you."

"Vanya?" Mariah's head was starting to spin. Speaking English didn't always mean the same thing.

"Ivan, my fiancé. I call him Vanya. He and I both believe a person should follow his heart. No matter the risk, that is where one should be."

"And Stash?"

"He is stubborn. He had this idea that we are going to follow him meekly back to America."

"But you did."

Tatiana studied the floor for a minute. Mariah was struck by the thickness of her lashes, so like her brother's.

"Stash wouldn't leave Russia without one of us. So I agreed. He was so unhappy there. Without you," she added. "But I am not here forever. I visit. Then I return to my husband-to-be and my mother."

"Does Stash know this?"

"He doesn't believe I have such a will of my own. You see, I was fourteen when he left. I have grown up. He will learn."

Mariah smiled. Tatiana's soft voice hid an iron backbone.

Mariah sipped her coffee, hiding a grin. The family resemblance extended to autocractic ways. "About your mother . . ."

"In the home, she rules. Stash knows that. She will bless him when he returns, but she won't leave Moscow."

"And if Stash won't leave without her?"

Tatiana lifted her head like a czarina. "My mother didn't suffer all these years to see her son give up his career."

Both women smiled slowly. "He doesn't stand a chance," Mariah murmured.

Twelve

Premature congratulations, that's what Mariah called them. She'd run a gauntlet of smiles and thumbs-ups as she rushed down the hall to the dressing room thirty minutes before the premiere began. Her nerves were as shredded as her first pair of tights. Wadding them up with a curse, she quickly borrowed another pair from Constanza.

It wasn't just that she'd be putting herself on the line that night, dancing for a phalanx of New York critics. Or that the company she'd built was on the same line. Or that Stash would be dancing for *them* tonight. It was all of that and then some. Her whole life depended on this.

Should a little thing like that make a woman nervous?

She and Stash had spent six nights together. She woke beside him, shared showers with him, ate breakfast with him and Tatiana. He was supportive, encouraging, and understanding—a woman's dream. The way he drew the press freed up time for her to work on the last details of the performance.

But once the premiere was done, she'd have no hold on him. Honoring that commitment was as far as his loyalty stretched.

Mariah joined Stash in the wings for warm-up. He kissed her warmly and was just about to speak when Tatiana rushed down the hall, parting the milling dancers.

She looked even more striking since Stash had bought her a new wardrobe—Guess jeans, a silk blouse, and a full-length fur. Shameless bribes, all of them.

"Am I late?" Tatiana asked.

"Thirty seconds to curtain," the stage manager said.

"Right on time," Mariah replied, glancing at Stash.

He touched her shoulder. "Be good."

It sounded too much like good-bye for a heart-stopping moment. She smiled bravely, though her confidence tottered. "I plan on it."

The lights were going down out front, the hum of conversation dwindling.

Mariah walked out onstage to the knot of dancers already there and put her arms around a few shoulders. Hugs. Pats. Thumbs-up. Emotion given and shared. Stash stayed in the wings, watching her, feeling the knife twist slowly in his heart. She'd survive without him.

The dancers broke from their football-style huddle and took up their positions. The music began. The curtain slowly rose. Stash heard Mariah's softly spoken words, meant only for her dancers. "Here we are, world."

Stash and Shelly danced after the ensemble number. Then Danny in a solo and Shelly in hers. Intermission came and went in a flurry of costume changes and revised lighting cues. Mariah wanted perfection. She wanted Stash. She'd told him, but the time was rapidly approaching to show him. She hoped and prayed she knew how.

The second half began with her solo, *Since I Fell for You*. Could she say it any clearer? Her longing cut through the lights, the distance, like the heat lightning of a gathering storm. She didn't dare look into the wings, although every trembling inch of her knew he was there. How could he not see how much she needed him?

Stash's glittering gaze fixed on her as he stood offstage in his white tunic and black tights. His arms crossed, he didn't move so much as a muscle. He knew every step of this dance as well as he knew every part of her body, every curve. It was as if she were dancing inside him, in his blood. But like their tender and furious lovemaking this week, each move was new, imbued with need and aching loneliness. No more the optimistic ending, no more her reaching out. She wrapped her arms around herself as the spotlight shrank and merely held on. Love scorned, deserted. He'd taught her that pain.

It was up to him to erase it, but how?

The dance ended. She rushed off, brushing past him, blinded by tears.

Tatiana took Stash's arm, preventing him from following her into the dressing room. "What a hard time you must be having. Loving three women, all of them with their own opinions."

"Tatiana, don't start."

But his sister was laughing, lightly and gaily, careful not to be heard beyond the wings as the ensemble did their next number.

Stash remembered that laugh. Also the devlish twinkle in his sister's eye. She'd been little more than a child when he left. "You suffered a lot because of me."

Tatiana shrugged a distinctly Russian shrug. "A person would be awfully naive to expect a life with no hardship."

"I intend to make it up to you. No hassles here, no interrogations, no one opening your mail."

"No one holding me in bed."

Stash snorted and turned away. Hard as it was to envision his sister as a woman, it was harder to give her up to a man he'd met only twice. "I'll come back to Russia and look after you."

"And you and Vanya will fight."

True. The young hothead refused to see things Stash's way, and he was practically living in the Moscow apartment. Housing shortage, he claimed. Bah!

Stash glared at the eight dancers doing eight different things and all of it working in delicate unison because Mariah made it so.

When he glanced back at Tatiana, she was forming a make-believe camera with her fingers and snapping a picture. "If you could see the look of love on your face when you watch her dance, you wouldn't speak all this nonsense."

"I love you too."

She popped up on her toes and gave him a hardy kiss on each cheek. "And we love you. You must come visit." This said, she bent to pick up the suitcase she'd leaned against a wall. "And I must catch my flight home."

"You will not go. You stay here!"

"I never promised, Petr."

"I insist."

"New York to Paris, then Berlin, then Moscow. You know it, you traveled it not long ago. Before coming back for Mariah."

"I brought *you* back here and I will bring Mama."

"You could have put me on the plane and stayed. You came yourself because of her. Don't think I'm dense, brother."

She was also getting him off the subject. Stash folded his arms; the Cossack resemblance multiplied tenfold in the white tunic. "That doesn't mean I'll let you leave."

"Where Ivan lives, Stash, I live. I'm going."

And he thought American women were headstrong. "This is what I get for leaving you with Mama."

"She is proud of you. Very proud." Her smile was bright. "She will watch you from there, as she always has."

He opened his mouth, then stopped. If he'd stayed in Russia, would he be strong enough to watch Mariah from the same distance?

The ensemble number was half over when Danny knocked on the dressing room door. "Mariah? Seen Stash?"

Mariah's heart rate tripled. She knew Tatiana was planning a hasty return to Moscow that night. Stash wouldn't have followed her, would he? Making a mental note of the point in the music, she knew she had five minutes to find him before they were scheduled to go on. Calling to Danny to be ready to dance in place of Stash, she rushed down the hall.

The stage door was open, a taxi idling in the alley outside. Stash was shouting orders in Russian at the cab driver. Tatiana was leaning out the window. She'd reserved a fierce hug for Mariah.

"I'm sorry you couldn't stay for the whole show," Mariah said.

"I am so happy for you, sister. He loves you, you know. I thought someday he would come home, but . . ." Tatiana caressed Mariah's cheek with her palm, an intimate family gesture. "Now I see his home is here.

"Anyway," Tatiana added as Stash shoved dollar bills at the driver, "my mother would be just as happy if he settled down. All these starlets." She dismissed them with a wave of her hand. "He should get a wife worthy of him."

Mariah was tugged forward so hard, she almost tumbled through the taxi window as Tatiana kissed her on both cheeks. "You bring him to visit Vanya and me!"

"I will. I've been thinking The Movement might tour Russia."

"My brother would like. He likes to show up."

"Show off."

Tatiana smiled and waved gaily to them both as the taxi pulled away.

Mariah looked at Stash's scowling face. Hope and nervousness fluttered within her. "We're on next," she said, her throat dry. "Any minute now."

"You knew she was going."

Mariah looked after the taillights as they disappeared around the corner. "Seems leaving quickly runs in your family."

His scowl deepened. Maybe he deserved that one. "She'll miss our dance." *Ours*, he thought fiercely as he followed Mariah through the wings.

"She's seen it on tape."

Applause thundered in the theater, giving them a few moments while the ensemble took their bows.

What good was videotape? Stash thought. Mariah's choreography was part of him, memorized on his skin, in his muscles, his bones, this ache in his chest that wouldn't go away. Could tape duplicate that? Would she use it to teach new partners how to touch her like he did, move with her like he did?

No. Those dances were *made* for him. Ego rushed in to blot out the pain. Tape couldn't hold her the way he could, feeling her ribs expand, the bunch of her muscles, sinewy and elongated, the tangy smell of her skin.

He took his place onstage after the curtain came down. Mariah nodded to the stage manager.

She wasn't prepared, she thought with a flash of panic in that hushed moment before the curtain rose. How many rehearsals could have prepared her for this? She felt Stash's body beside her, his heat, his energy, and could do no more than concentrate on one loose thread hanging off the blue velvet curtain as it rose with a creak and a whirl of gears.

"Here we are, world," Stash whispered for her ears only. With grim satisfaction he felt her shudder. The music began and they started to move.

It was an announcement of their love. He made

that clear from the first. Let the curious look. Let the world know they were a couple. Sensuality, need, and desire mixed. Yes, it was rehearsed, but no less real. Soaked with emotion, the dance continued, the heat from the lights laying on their skin like a rumpled sheet. There wasn't a moment when he wasn't touching her.

She'd designed it that way.

This had been her plan, Mariah reminded herself. To show him her love, to make it so clear he couldn't deny it. But he'd swooped in and caught her off balance, pulling her into his arms and making her his for all to see. She was the one being claimed. He was branding the part his and the woman with it.

Meanwhile there were beats to listen for, pauses, lyrics dimly heard, something about learning how to tell someone good-bye. There were precious few moments left to hold him. A step, a turn, and it was over. He was dragging her into his arms for one long, last kiss.

The spotlight stayed on them. The roaring in her ears was more than the audience's applause. The mouth on hers was Stash's, greedy, hungry, unappeasable. The curtain was halfway down when he threw his head back and speared her with his gaze.

"No one will ever dance this with you." A command.

"No one."

Somehow they were backstage again. Mariah felt as if she were in pieces. Her stomach churned, her palms were clammy, her head spun. People were clapping her on the back, and she was being hugged by every dancer in her company.

Stash parted the crowd. "Excuse please, people." He wrapped an arm around her shoulders.

She wanted to ask where he was taking her, when he was leaving, and why. Above all, why? But he'd slipped into his impresario persona. He marched her through the throng and opened a door.

"We talk."

The broom closet.

She bumped a shin on the mop bucket. "Stash—"

"This is where we start; this is where we finish."

Finish. She'd failed. She hadn't gotten him to stay, hadn't found the words or the music.

He crowded in beside her. "I am the greatest dancer in the world, no?"

She didn't answer, couldn't. Was that the only statement he'd been making? Claiming the part but not the partner?

Stash studied her. Her lashes were dark with mascara. He liked them pale brown. And he liked her hair down. Tight like this it revealed her face, not her soul. He wanted the woman naked, the illusions dispensed with.

"Here, we take out these pins." He tugged at them, and they hit the mop bucket with a tinny ping. "I lied to you."

If he had, she didn't want to hear it. "Not now."

"Now. Then. Here. I said I wanted to dance with you."

"Dance naked."

He smiled, a sad smile. "At least that much was true. But I let you think it was mostly to dance with you that I came here."

"Now we've danced."

"I wanted your body and your Movement."

"You've had it," she said, a little angry, heat flushing her cheeks. The adrenaline of the performance was zinging through her bloodstream, careening off uncertainty and decisions only he could make. The premiere was over. Where did that leave them? "If you're going, just tell me."

Brave Mariah, he thought. "The firing squad without the blindfold, eh?"

"I believe in honesty."

"And I haven't always given it to you. Forgive me."

She'd rather love him. "Stash, I've told you. I know how much your family means to you. I can't blame you for loving them—" *More than me*, she almost added.

"But you want to talk me out of going."

"Only because they're all right without you. You don't see that."

Perhaps not, he admitted silently, but onstage he'd seen all he needed to in a sudden brilliant light, as bright as the follow spot, as suffused and gentle and certain as the dawn. He was meant to dance with her, to love her. This time there'd be no looking back.

"You've been so focused on rescuing them, you never saw they'd managed," Mariah tried again.

"I see that." What he saw were her eyes, brown and warm and wide. However he managed to deal with his family, she would be at his side. It was the only way. He put a finger to her lips as she came up with another argument. "Hush, we don't need to talk anymore."

Her eyes narrowed. "Oh, no?"

She wanted to stalk, pace, lecture. She wanted

to curl up in his arms and cry. "Stash, don't clam up on me. Tell me what you're feeling."

"We danced what I was feeling. Didn't you know?"

In every molecule of her being. "But I have to hear it. A woman has to hear some things sometimes." Even if it's good-bye.

It took Stash a few moments to gather the words.

"I insist on new contract," he said finally. "I wish to make this legal."

She fought down the flare of hope that refused to die. The look in his eyes, the smile at the corner of his mouth, didn't help. "'Making it legal' is a phrase I think I should explain, Stash. In English it has what they call certain connotations."

"It means contract, like marriage contract."

A hush fell over her heart. "Yes, it does."

"Then I am saying it right."

His kiss said it even righter. Long, deep, open to the pain of renewed hope, the rekindled ashes of dreams feared dead. "Mariah, love."

She looked up into his eyes, her heart beating quick and joyful. The bare light bulb shone slickly off his hair. Its harsh glow didn't matter. The smell of disinfectant didn't matter. The bundles of brown paper towels on gray metal shelving, the concrete block walls, that mop handle poking under her arm—none of it mattered. It was the most romantic place in the world.

"As for my knee . . ."

She swallowed, rueing all the times she'd told herself she'd have him as long as he could dance and that would be enough. "Stash, I can't go through all of this if you're going to leave eventually. I know you came here to dance."

"Then I still haven't said it right. In the contract I want the phrase, in sickness and in health."

"You mean it?"

"Even when I said it wrong, I've always meant it. I love you. That is right, yes?"

"Yes."

She threw herself into his arms.

After savoring her mouth, her body, her love, he asked "Ready?" He nodded toward the door. "Is settled? I teach male dancers, you choreograph, we work together. I also am spokesman for company when you are busy. And you wear my dancewear."

"A real partnership."

"In all senses."

She had trouble thinking of any senses beyond smell, taste, touch, and sound. So real, so achingly real. "Capitalism, look out," she managed with a smile.

"Dance companies are not cheap. We need money, we get it."

"We'll need each other, and that's all we'll ever need."

"You say it better than I do."

He leaned her against the door to kiss her again, bodies aligned, arms twined. In a corner of her mind Mariah wondered if that doorknob was still broken and if they'd be in there all night. It didn't seem to matter.

Then the door popped open and they tumbled backward into the hallway. Some fancy footwork on Stash's part prevented them from sprawling at Shelly's feet.

"Hi, guys."

"Hello!" Stash swiped a lock of hair off his forehead. With a flourish he bowed deeply. "I wish to introduce you as first to hear, to new partnership."

"Dancing partners?" Shelly asked, brows raised.

"Dancing, business, life, everything."

"About time," she muttered, resolutely unimpressed. She went up on pointe to plant a kiss on Stash's cheek. "It was fun dancing with you."

"You'll still dance together," Mariah insisted. "just not in everything."

"Looks like she's still the boss," Shelly added.

"In The Movement, yes," Stash agreed.

Peering over his shoulder into the broom closet, Shelly winked saucily at them both before heading toward the dressing room. "Piece of advice, Stash," she called over her shoulder. "If you're gonna be around much longer, I'd demand a bigger office."

Thirteen

"You are the greatest man, dancer, lover in the world. How's that?" Mariah wrapped her arms around Stash's neck and kissed him for all she was worth. Exactly what she should have done the first time they'd walked into that broom closet, but her pride hadn't let her flat-out adore the man. Until now.

They stood by the window of his corner apartment, looking down on a darkened Central Park. Misty paths cut through the trees like rivers of light.

The phone had finally stopped ringing. The telegrams were being held by the doorman.

"You see, Mariah," he said, gesturing at the window, "the city is awake because we need it to sparkle for us. It is like that for lovers."

She shook her head. Her hair, soft and fine and feathery, was the color of russet and honey, as precious to Stash as gold. Her cheeks were still highlighted by pale fire. He'd begun making love to her as soon as the last guest left the post-premiere party. Their own party was just beginning. "Why do you shake your head?"

"You're such a romantic," she replied.

"A true Russian."

"I should have known you were staying all along."

"How could you when I was too thick to see it myself?"

"I should have realized when you let Tatiana go."

"I did that because I couldn't paddle her behind in public. I should have known she'd go. I was being stubborn, pigheaded. Or is it big-headed?"

"Maybe both," she said, grinning.

He wound his arms around her waist from behind, feeling the coolness of the glass as they looked out on the lights winking off across the city.

"When I was over there, I couldn't stop thinking of you." He pressed her body against his and had to say it, had to put these feelings into words for both their sakes. "It made me crazy, being there, knowing you were here and I might never touch you again. Like a wolf in a trap, I didn't know where to turn." He could still feel that clutching in his gut, the need to escape, not *from* this time, but *to*.

"I see how my mother must have suffered when I first left, but that was like a bird letting its young fly away. It's different with a man and woman. It took me a world to find you and no world was going to separate us."

"You came back."

"The Red Army couldn't have kept me there."

"Only your own stubbornness."

"And my family's."

Mariah took a deep breath and sighed. Her skin still warm from their lovemaking, a slow thrumming heat remained where he touched her. "Maybe we'll go back together and dance for them."

"For the wedding of Tatiana and Ivan."

"For peace and freedom." She twisted in his arms to face him. "Not to mention the triumph of love."

Looking into her eyes, he knew it was true.

She chuckled coyly and batted her lashes at him. "It's a long way to take me home to meet your mother."

"It is proper. When we come back we work hard, make love, even make babies."

"Maybe."

"Love, dance, and work. This is life, no?"

"This is life, yes."

They met halfway, a deep kiss, a deeper promise.

"Ahem. May I come up for air now?" Mariah gasped.

He was crushing her to him. Nevertheless, he let her go only far enough so he could frame her face in his hands, kiss each cheek, her forehead, her nose, her eyelids.

"Keep trying and you'll find my mouth," she teased.

"If I do, our window-gazing is over for the night."

"To the bedroom?"

"To the bedroom." There was a view there, too, though they'd spent little time seeing it.

"I will show you the Northern Lights," he whispered, "the white nights."

"Your home."

"My home is here."

No words had ever sounded more perfect. "Your

English is getting better all the time. By leaps and bounds."

He ran a hand down her side, heard her soft gasp in reply.

"Speaking of leaps," she managed to say, "there was this character named Icarus. He flew to the sun. Like you, daring, leaping."

"And?"

"Take me there, Stash. Take me to the sun."

In the living room music still played. In the bedroom, dark and heated, they danced their private dance.

THE EDITOR'S CORNER

What a joy it is to see, hear, smell and touch spring once again! Like a magician, nature is pulling splendors out of an invisible hat—and making us even more aware of romance. To warm you with all the radiance and hopefulness of the season, we've gathered together a bouquet of six fabulous LOVESWEPTs.

First, from the magical pen of Mary Kay McComas, we have **KISS ME, KELLY,** LOVESWEPT #462. Kelly has a rule about dating cops—she doesn't! But Baker is a man who breaks the rules. In the instant he commands her to kiss him he seizes control of her heart—and dares her to tell him she doesn't want him as much as he wants her. But once Kelly has surrendered to the ecstasy he offers, can he betray that passion by seducing her to help him with a desperate, dirty job? A story that glows with all the excitement and uncertainties of true love.

With all things green and beautiful about to pop into view, we bring you talented Gail Douglas's **THE BEST LAID PLANS,** LOVESWEPT #463. Jennifer Allan has greenery *and* beauty on her mind as she prepares to find out exactly what Clay Parrish, an urban planner, intends to do to her picturesque hometown. Clay is a sweet-talker with an irrepressible grin, and in a single sizzling moment he breaches Jennifer's defenses. Once he begins to understand her fears, he wages a glorious campaign to win her trust. A lot of wooing . . . and a lot of magic—in a romance you can't let yourself miss.

In Texas spring comes early, and it comes on strong— and so do the hero and heroine of Jan Hudson's **BIG AND BRIGHT,** LOVESWEPT #464. Holt Berringer is one of the good guys, a long lean Texas Ranger with sin-black eyes and a big white Stetson. When the entrancing spitfire Cory Bright has a run-in with some bad guys, Holt admires her refusal to hide from threats on her life and is determined to cherish and protect her. Cory fears he will be too much like the domineering macho men she's grown to dislike, but Holt is as tender as he is tough. Once Cory proves that she can make it on her own, will she be brave enough to settle for the man she really wants? A double-barrelled delight from the land of yellow roses.

Peggy Webb's **THAT JONES GIRL**, LOVESWEPT #465, is a marvelous tale about the renewal of an old love between a wild Irish rover and a beautiful singer. Brawny wanderer Mick Flannigan had been Tess Jones's first lover, best friend, and husband—until the day years before when he suddenly left her. Now destiny has thrown them together again, but Tess is still too hot for Mick to handle. She draws him like a magnet, and he yearns to recapture the past, to beg Tess's forgiveness . . . but can this passion that has never died turn into trust? For Peggy's many fans, here is a story that is as fresh, energetic, and captivating as a spring morning.

Erica Spindler's enchanting **WISHING MOON**, LOVE-SWEPT #466, features a hero who gives a first impression that belies the real man. Lance Alexander seems to be all business, whether he is hiring a fund-raiser for his favorite charity or looking for a wife. When he runs into the cocky and confident Madi Muldoon, she appears to be the last person he would choose to help in the fight to save the sea turtles—until she proves otherwise and he falls under the spell of her tawny-eyed beauty. Still Lance finds it hard to trust in any woman's love, while Madi thinks she has lost her faith in marriage. Can they both learn that wishes made on a full moon—especially wishes born of an irresistible love for each other—always come true? A story as tender and warm as spring itself.

In April the world begins to move outdoors again and it's time to have a little fun. That's what brings two lovers together in Marcia Evanick's delightful **GUARDIAN SPIRIT**, LOVESWEPT #467. As a teenager Josh Langly had been the town bad boy; now he is the local sheriff. When friends pair him with the bewitching dark-haired Laura Ann Bryant for the annual scavenger hunt, the two of them soon have more on their minds than the game.

Forced by the rules to stay side by side with Josh for a weekend, Laura is soon filled with a wanton desire for this good-guy hunk with the devilish grin. And though Josh is trying to bury his bad boy past beneath a noble facade, Laura enchants him beyond all reason and kindles an old flame. Another delectable treat from Marcia Evanick.

And (as if this weren't enough!) be sure not to miss three unforgettable novels coming your way in April from Bantam's spectacular new imprint, FANFARE, featuring the best in women's popular fiction. First, for the many fans of Deborah Smith, we have her deeply moving and truly memorable historical **BELOVED WOMAN**. This is the glorious story of a remarkable Cherokee woman, Katherine Blue Song, and an equally remarkable frontiersman Justis Gallatin. Then, making her debut with FANFARE, Jessica Bryan brings you a spellbinding historical fantasy, **ACROSS A WINE-DARK SEA**. This story has already wowed *Rendezvous* magazine, which called Jessica Bryan "a super storyteller" and raved about the book, describing it as "different, exciting, excellent . . ." The critically-acclaimed Virginia Brown takes readers back to the wildest days of the Wild West for a fabulous and heartwarming love story in **RIVER'S DREAM**.

All in all, a terrific month of reading in store for you from FANFARE and LOVESWEPT!

Sincerely,

Carolyn Nichols

Carolyn Nichols,
Publisher,
LOVESWEPT
Bantam Books
666 Fifth Avenue
New York, NY 10103

60 Minutes to a Better, More Beautiful You!

Now it's easier than ever to awaken your sensuality, stay slim forever—even make yourself irresistible. With Bantam's bestselling subliminal audio tapes, you're only 60 minutes away from a better, more beautiful you!

__ 45004-2	**Slim Forever**	$8.95
__ 45035-2	**Stop Smoking Forever**	$8.95
__ 45022-0	**Positively Change Your Life**	$8.95
__ 45041-7	**Stress Free Forever**	$8.95
__ 45106-5	**Get a Good Night's Sleep**	$7.95
__ 45094-8	**Improve Your Concentration**	$7.95
__ 45172-3	**Develop A Perfect Memory**	$8.95

Bantam Books, Dept. LT, 414 East Golf Road, Des Plaines, IL 60016

Please send me the items I have checked above. I am enclosing $_____ (please add $2.50 to cover postage and handling). Send check or money order, no cash or C.O.D.s please. (Tape offer good in USA only.)

Mr/Ms _____

Address _____

City/State _____ Zip _____

LT-2/91

Please allow four to six weeks for delivery.
Prices and availability subject to change without notice.

NEW!
Handsome Book Covers Specially Designed To Fit Loveswept Books

Our new French Calf Vinyl book covers come in a set of three great colors— royal blue, scarlet red and kachina green.

Each 7" × 9½" book cover has two deep vertical pockets, a handy sewn-in bookmark, and is soil and scratch resistant.

To order your set, use the form below.